Like so many introverts, Laure has a secret persona online — one who writes romance. Every Saturday night, she gets comfortable with her blanket, her tea, and her laptop, and reads and writes love stories to her heart's content.

In real life, she has a crush on her colleague Denis. She'd love to be as forward and adventurous as her characters and flirt with the guy, but her shyness stops her from doing more than asking for his help on correcting today's bug.

Everything is going along just fine — until her two worlds start to overlap.

Hiding in Plain Sight

A French Office Romance

R.W. WALLACE

Hiding in Plain Sight
by R.W. Wallace

Copyright © 2020 by R.W. Wallace

Copy editing by Wendy Janes
Cover Illustration 112324184 © Roman Samborskyi | 123rf.com
Cover Illustration 109932412 © greens87 | 123rf.com
Cover by the author

All characters and events in this book, other than those clearly in the public domain, are fictitious and any resemblance to real persons, living or dead, is purely coincidental.

This book was first published in 2020 under the author name Eva Saint-Julien.

All rights reserved. No part of this publication may be reproduced, distributed, or transmitted in any form or by any means, including photocopying, recording, or other electronic or mechanical methods, without the prior written permission of the publisher, except in the case of brief quotations embodied in critical reviews and certain other noncommercial uses permitted by copyright law.

www.rwwallace.com

ISBN: [979-10-95707-66-0]

Main category—Fiction
Other category—Romance

First Edition

Don't miss the first book in the French Office Romance Series:

Be sure to define the rules before you play...

Tristan will come out to his colleagues when he meets the right guy. He just hasn't met him yet.

Fidi, out and proud, plays a game with his colleagues to prove that they treat him differently because of his sexuality.

But what happens when someone doesn't play by the rules?

ONE

What More Could a Girl Want on a Saturday Night?

I SNUGGLED INTO my favorite—and only—chair, my legs crossed so I was sitting on my feet, the bright pink cover my mother had given me as a housewarming gift when I first moved away from home to start my engineering studies covering me from head to toe, and my tiny laptop/tablet/TV in my lap.

I let out a *whee* to myself as I opened the writing forum and saw I had fifteen new comments on my latest chapter.

My mother kept pushing me to get a "real" apartment now that I had a job and an actual income. She couldn't fathom why I'd want to stay in my studio close to campus when I could easily afford a one-room in the city center.

I didn't see the point in living in the city center—I'm two minutes away from a metro station and can be on the Place du Capitole in twenty minutes.

Why on earth would I need an extra room just to put my bed in? I was all alone here and never felt like inviting anyone into my space—that would require way too much cleaning up and removing the evidence of my secret little passion.

In twenty-five square meters I had everything I needed: a small kitchenette to cook; a single bed that could double as a couch if I felt like pretending like I was an adult; a desk that I was thinking about getting rid of now that I didn't have homework anymore; and my chair.

This was where I spent all my time. Chair, cover, laptop, and I was all set.

Actually, on second thought, I might need to keep the desk. It was the only place I could set down my cup of tea when I was sitting in my chair.

I clicked on my latest chapter to get to the comments.

Tinkerbell98 was the first one out, as usual. Seriously, this girl must have had an alert set on all my stories and opened and read every new chapter within minutes. This comment came in fifteen minutes after the chapter went live.

Tinkerbell98: Love *how this is moving along!!! Can't wait to see what happens when they find themselves alone!!!*

I grinned as I counted the exclamation points. It was generally a good indicator of how much she liked a story. So far, my maximum was for a sex scene in my previous story, where she fit a total of twenty-six exclamation points into a three-line comment.

This was only the third chapter of a story, so six exclamation points was pretty good.

I scrolled through the other comments, clicking the thumbs-up icon for every single one, so they'd know I'd seen it.

Three quarters of the way down, I stopped scrolling and broke into a huge grin.

> **DD**: *Love what you're doing here, Lily. We're only three chapters in and I already feel like I've known your heroine for years. Seems like the kind of girl I'd want to be friends with. And I definitely want her to find love! Will we be getting Eric's point of view in the next chapter? I can't wait to find out how he's seeing her!*

I clicked the thumbs-up icon, my whole body lighting up at the praise.

I went through the rest of the comments, but my mind was already on the private message I'd send DD.

I'd always loved stories, of course. My parents read me bedtime stories from day one, even when I didn't understand a word, and kept at it until I was ten. Then I realized I could read faster on my own, so I sent my dad packing and settled in under my covers as soon as my homework was done, only agreeing to turn off the light when my mom used her I'm-one-warning-away-from-getting-angry voice.

Unsurprisingly, I loved Harry Potter. Who didn't?

But the problem with Harry Potter was that there were only seven books, and then you're done. Sure, I re-read them so many times I could probably give you a scene-by-scene description of the entire series, but it's not the same as discovering the stories for the first time.

Enter fanfiction.

One day during my last year of high school, I was surfing the net looking for something to distract me when I was supposed to be working on my biology homework.

I must have been searching for something Harry Potter related. On the second page of hits, I found the title of a story.

A love story between Ginny and Harry.

At first I was outraged that someone would take Rowling's characters and *use* them like that. Have them do stuff that would *not* be okay with the younger part of the Harry Potter fandom.

But I also couldn't stop reading.

The author had Harry down pat. Ginny was lively and lovable.

The writing was awesome.

So chapter after chapter, I kept clicking on to the next one, my annoyance at the author for using my favorite characters slipping away.

At two in the morning, I still hadn't done my biology homework and I'd finished reading a fifty-thousand-word novel.

Fanfiction quickly became my new passion.

I read everything by the first author I found. Then I discovered the website the story was on specialized in fanfiction and had *thousands* of stories in the Harry Potter universe.

They were sorted by *pairings*.

All the stories were love stories, in one form or another.

How had I reached the age of eighteen without ever reading a romance? By reading the types of books my parents read, that's how. I got cozy mysteries and women's fiction from my mom, and horror, fantasy, and hardboiled mysteries from my dad. Romance was simply an element of many of the stories, but never the main focus.

So I spent a lot of time on the fanfiction website, reading every Ginny/Harry and Ron/Hermione story I could find. And

I filled my Kindle with romance books from authors I realized were international bestsellers even though I'd never heard of them before.

Honestly, it's a miracle I got acceptable grades when I graduated high school. It was a good thing I was a natural at math and physics.

But right now it was Saturday night, and I didn't need to think about math, programming, or work for another thirty hours at least.

I opened the private messages and clicked in to the conversation I had going with DD. It had two hundred and thirty-six messages.

> **Lily**: *Thank you so much for the awesome comment on my last chapter! I'm glad you liked it. You putting up your next chapter tonight, as usual? I can't wait to see what Laure and Fred will be like in bed. I bet it'll be hot as hell!*
>
> *I'm really impressed by how you've made me fall in love with Fred, by the way. At first he was a real jackass and I honestly didn't know if I'd want to read an entire book with him in it. I know it's a really common trope, to have the jackass fall in love and become a nice guy, and it's not my favorite romance, usually.*
>
> *But right from the go, when we got into Fred's head in the second chapter, I was wowed. He's a jackass on the outside, but so, so sweet on the inside. Laure doesn't need to change him, she only needs to make him understand it's okay to be himself!*
>
> *Seriously, looking forward to the sex scene that just better be in your next chapter!*
>
> *Lily*

At first, it had felt weird to read a story where the heroine had the same name as me. Especially since she could *sort of* be described to resemble me. Sort of. If you took me and made me super beautiful. You know, dark blond hair that reflected the sun, large soulful eyes, and a perfect nose, instead of dark blond hair that took twenty minutes to comb every morning, large uninteresting eyes, and a pointy nose.

Anyway, my online friend's heroine had the same name as real-life me, and it had been weird at first. Until the romantic interest turned out to be scorching hot, smart, and a guy I really wanted to get to know—and then I just went with it and lived that wonderful love story as if it was my own.

The first sex scene was coming up.

I just knew it.

I had my relaxing herbal tea, my warm cover, my online friend, and a great story to look forward to.

What more could a girl want on a Saturday night?

TWO

A Half-Naked Hunk on the Cover

As I combed my hair on Monday morning, I kept reliving DD's latest chapter. I tried to figure out why it was so satisfying.

There hadn't even been any sex!

Again with the clichés, the lovers were interrupted by the roommate coming home earlier than expected and the characters—and the readers—had been left hanging.

But it was so damned well-written! I re-read the chapter three times over the weekend and couldn't put my finger on why it had been so great.

It made me feel all warm and gushy inside.

Once my hair was free of knots, I opened the left-hand cupboard over my sink. The right-hand side had all the classic bathroom stuff like toothbrush, toothpaste, creams, makeup remover.

The left was for my barrettes.

My mom bought me my first flower barrette on a trip to Italy when I was ten. The flower was cheap plastic and the clip of the barrette hadn't survived more than a week in the busy schoolyard, but it was the beginning of a long string of decorations for me to put in my hair.

I loved the way the flowers looked on the side of my head. How it drew the attention away from my face. How they made me think of warm and exotic places I'd only read about.

At this point in time, I had about fifteen different barrettes. Different colors. Different sizes. Different types of flowers.

The lilies were my favorites.

Since I'd gone with a pair of jeans and a light, flowing white top, I chose the white lily. I attached my hair above my right ear, put on some mascara, and I was ready to go to work.

I just had to send *one* more message first.

Lily: *Come on, DD. Won't you please share the next chapter with me? I have to know what happens next! You can't make me wait until next Saturday! That's like six days away! I know you have at least five more chapters written.*

Shoving my phone into my back pocket, I grabbed my purse by the door and left for work.

I received my answer as I got out of my car at work.

DD: *I'll have you know I have the whole story finished! But you're going to have to wait for the next chapter like everybody else. Why don't you spend your energy thinking about your own story, instead. Like figuring out how to sell the balding guy* *as a sexy romantic interest. I'm not sure I've ever seen anyone pull that one off before.*

Tutting at my phone, I tap in an answer as I walk blindly toward the office building's main entrance.

Lily: *I'm disappointed, DD. I really didn't think you'd be that superficial. Please don't tell me you've never read a romance book that doesn't have a half-naked hunk on the cover! I've read plenty of books where the hero can't be described as, "even his muscles had muscles." Why should whether or not he has a headfull of hair make any difference?*

Besides, it's all part of my plan—but you'll have to wait for a chapter or two more to see!

Unless you'd like to exchange the rest of your story for the rest of mine?

I slipped my phone into my purse and pulled my badge out of it. Opening the turnstiles next to the receptionist's desk, I pulled the lanyard over my head, taking care not to touch the barrette.

My phone pinged.

DD: *Nice try! I'll have to be patient, I guess, to figure out how a balding twenty-eight-year-old can be considered sexy.*

For once, I didn't tap out a reply immediately. As I made my way toward my office, I frowned as I mulled over my friend's words.

I liked a physically perfect specimen of a man as well as the next girl, but looks really weren't everything. In fact, lately, I'd gotten quite tired of the stories of cold, gorgeous billionaires who just needed the right girl to realize they needed love and someone to share their limitless fortune with.

I mean, that would *never* happen in real life.

I enjoyed stories like DD's, where I could imagine being the heroine, imagine it being me falling in love.

And I couldn't see myself with someone with a perfectly sculpted body.

I didn't think I was fat, or particularly ugly, mind. I just wasn't—let's go with I wouldn't win any beauty contests.

And I was fine with that.

Also, to get those perfect bodies, those guys must be working out every single day. I couldn't imagine living with someone and then lounge in my chair in front of my computer while he spent hours lifting weights.

I'd feel guilty for not doing the same. I'd probably get tired simply looking at him working out.

Nope, give me a normal guy any day. It's possible to be attractive without being a mountain of muscles.

I shook myself out of my reverie as I entered the office I shared with three guys.

Tristan, the guy who'd taken over as Project Manager a week ago, looked up from his computer as I entered. "Morning," he said.

"Morning," I replied. I walked over to do *la bise*, a kiss on each cheek.

Tristan pointed to my desk in the corner. "You forgot to lock up your computer again." He didn't even look at me as he said it, clearly preoccupied with something on his own screen.

"It's attached with the cable," I replied as I moved on to greet Fidi, another new arrival.

"The cable can be cut in about two seconds if you have the right tools," Tristan replied.

I knew I should feel guilty or something for being criticized like this first thing in the morning, but the delivery was so half-hearted, I didn't think he'd actually remember doing it in ten minutes.

I moved on toward Denis, who sat in his usual fashion, leaning forward in his chair so his nose was way too close to his screen, one hand on the mouse and the other hovering over his keyboard, ready to type.

"What's the point in giving us cables if they're that easy to steal?" I mumbled to myself.

"Because it would be glaringly obvious," Denis said as he turned to do *la bise*, "if someone walked around here with tools like that in the middle of the day."

"Kiss-ass," I whispered, feeling my face heat up a little as I moved into his personal space. He smelled of aftershave and coffee. His scruff scratched as our chins touched.

I'd rather cut my own tongue out than admit it to anyone, but Denis was my main inspiration for the male character in my current story. The balding one.

Denis was twenty-eight and had worked on this team since he started his career four years ago. He was apparently some kind of programming genius, and had managed to impress even our new technical expert Fidi a time or two.

He was sweet, and smart, and funny once you managed to get him to open up a little.

He was at least as shy as me.

I had no idea what his type was. If he could possibly be interested in someone like me. I didn't even know if he liked girls.

For all I knew, he was fantasizing about Fidi—who was indisputably gorgeous, but also indisputably gay.

Nothing would ever happen, of course. There was no way I'd ever dare do *anything* that could indicate that I liked him.

But I could dream.

And I could write.

So my current work in progress was going to have a shy and quiet hero, with a balding head. I'd let my heroine have the romance I'd never work up the courage to take for myself.

What did DD know, anyway? Why shouldn't a guy who was well on his way to going bald in his twenties be allowed to find love?

I'd show her. Two more chapters—Tuesday and Thursday night—and she'd see what guys like Denis could do to a girl.

THREE

An Epiphany

DD: *You shaved his head! As if that would actually change anything. Now, don't get me wrong here, Lily. You know I love your writing and your characters. But thinking that shaving a guy's head will suddenly make him irresistible is just wishful thinking.*

Lily: *Not true! I know plenty of guys who look great with their heads shaved! And it doesn't matter if you can tell that they've done it because they were going bald—it makes them look… badass, for lack of a better word. They own it, you know?*

DD: *I'm not buying it. If the guy only looked passable before, shaving his head isn't going to change that.*

Lily: *Of course it doesn't change how he looks. But in this case, it made the heroine look at him in a new light. It made her not focus on the fact that he was balding. And I hope you noticed that she liked him before, too. She had an epiphany, of sorts. Instead of the retreating hairline drawing attention, you're drawn to the eyes. She's realizing he's gorgeous on the outside as well as inside.*

DD: *Hmm. I don't know. You're going to have to sell me on it in your story, I guess.*

Lily: *No problem. Challenge accepted!*

FOUR

I'll Help You Rub It In

It was Friday afternoon and we were all basically waiting for the clock to read five o'clock so we could go home for the weekend.

The day had been one of those beautiful spring gifts; startling blue sky, warm enough to wear only a summer dress but not so warm you had to seek out a shadow at all times, and chirping birds frolicking in the flowering trees. We'd kept our office window open to smell the spring but it mostly just made us regret ever getting a job that forced us to stay inside. We'd eaten our lunch sandwiches outside and Denis managed to get the beginnings of a sunburn at the back of his neck from that short hour out in the sun. It was the source of innumerable jokes all through the afternoon.

Now the sun sent lazy rays of light into our office, peeking through the blinds we were forced to lower partially in order to see our computer screens, highlighting the dust motes swirling around in a slow dance.

I stared at my screen, trying to make sense of the code I'd written that morning, trying to figure out why it didn't do what it should. At the point I was at, it was surprising it was doing anything at all, since it all seemed like gibberish.

When I was too tired, I forgot how to speak geek.

I'd stayed up way too late the night before, re-reading DD's previous story and chatting with her until my eyes closed of their own accord.

Shouldn't have done that, of course. I was a responsible adult who understood that work was for working and not for catching up on your sleep when you lost a night to internet activities.

At least, I was supposed to be.

Denis yawned as he stretched in his seat at his desk next to mine. At least I wasn't the only one suffering.

"Hey, Denis?" I said, figuring maybe we could try to keep each other awake for the remaining hour. "Would you mind having a look at this?" I pointed to my screen.

He let out a whooshing breath as he deflated from his stretch and his eyes met mine with a smile. "Sure."

He scooted his chair over next to mine and leaned his elbows on my desk, then propped his chin in his hand. "You on that 'undo' bug?"

My brain was still in slow motion, so instead of deciphering what his words meant, I studied his profile.

He had a tiny beauty mark on the left side of his nose, right in the fold. If he smiled, it would disappear from view. His jaw was covered in scruff—Denis seemed to shave once a week, during the weekend, so he'd be clean-shaven on Mondays and on the verge of qualifying for "bearded" on Fridays. I wondered how he looked on Sundays, if he tipped over into lumberjack territory or if he still looked like a geek who'd forgotten to shave. I wondered if the rest of him had a lot of hair—

Denis turned his head to face me, his sharp brown eyes meeting mine from less than thirty centimeters away. "What am I looking at?"

Me.

He was looking at me and I liked it.

"Uh…" I shook my head and squeezed my eyes shut. God, I shouldn't have called him over when my brain was at no more than twenty percent capacity.

"Rough afternoon, huh?" His voice was smooth and soft and understanding and I could hear his sweet smile.

Feeling myself blushing, I ran a hand over my face, which actually helped somewhat. "Gah. Didn't go to bed early enough last night," I said, my lips lifting in a self-deprecating smile. "Sorry."

Denis chuckled. "No worries. I'm in the same boat."

"Right." I took a deep breath and opened my eyes, taking care to look at my screen and not the delicious man leaning in close. "Yeah, I'm on the 'undo' bug. I managed to get it to undo the last action and not the before-last, but the background's still turning green. I have no idea why."

Finally, Denis turned his attention back to the computer, letting me breathe a little easier.

He hovered his hand over mine on the mouse. "Can I?"

Cursing myself for blushing yet again, this time because a frisson ran up my arm at feeling the heat of his hand over mine even if he never actually touched me, I removed my hand, letting him take over.

He stayed for twenty minutes, clicking around in my code, running plenty of tests, showing me the tools I could use to debug. He knew so much about coding, I was in awe of him every time he came over to help. To the point where I sometimes wondered what the hell I was doing in a job like this—I didn't stand a chance at ever reaching his level of expertise.

"There we go," he said as he relinquished the mouse and shoved the keyboard back in front of me. "No more green background."

"Thank you, Denis," I said, meeting his brown eyes and giving him a genuine smile. "That would have taken me a week—or forever—on my own."

A small blush crept into his cheeks, making him look adorable. "My pleasure, Laure. And, you know, it's also my job as Tech Lead." He broke eye contact, looking to my computer screen instead.

I was disappointed that his brown eyes left mine, but also oddly reassured that I wasn't the only one who had trouble keeping direct eye contact for more than a few seconds at a time.

He touched his neck and winced.

"You really managed to get sunburned, didn't you?" I said, grin in place.

His chuckle was a low rumble. "Apparently, yeah. I do this all the time, but I never learn."

He met my eyes again for a second before moving on to the window and presumably the beautiful, blue sky. Running a hand through his hair, a gleam appeared in his eyes. "At least I didn't burn my scalp. That's always a fun reminder that your hair's thinning away."

I was never quite sure how to react to this type of comment from a guy. It was usually a bit of a sore subject, but since he was the one to bring it up, and the tone stayed light and joking, I figured he was okay with me playing along.

"Getting old sucks, huh?" I added in a wink to make sure he knew I was joking.

He leaned back in his chair and swung from side to side as he grinned. "Totally. Twenty-eight is like already having a foot in the grave, basically."

Awesome, I'd read him correctly.

"I can't even imagine," I teased. "I guess you've looked into retirement options already, right? Maybe planned your funeral?"

His grin stretched into a full-blown smile, taking over his entire face and transforming him into something out of a dream.

"At least I should plan my brother's funeral first," he said. "He's two years older." He raised a finger and waggled his eyebrows. "And he was bald at twenty-two!"

I gasped and held a hand to my chest. "Oh, no! He might as well become a hermit if that's the case. His social life will be as good as dead if he doesn't have *hair*!"

"He *has* hair." Denis tipped his head from side to side. "But nothing north of the ears, that's all."

I gaped at him. "He has one of those monk-like haircuts? Why?!"

Denis shrugged, clearly amused by my reaction. "I don't know. Haven't asked him. It can be a bit of a touchy subject, you know."

"He should totally shave everything off," I said, thinking back on my conversation with DD. Was I having that much of a fixation on guys with a bald head, to manage to always turn all discussions in that direction?

"You think so?" Denis' smile was still present, but dialed down as he studied me. "You don't even know what he looks like."

My heart sped up as I worried I would insult him or his brother. Thinning hair *could* be a really touchy subject with some guys and I really hated confrontations. And I *really* didn't want to offend Denis in any way.

Still, in for a penny…

I met his eyes, making sure he could see I meant no offense. "I have yet to see a guy who rocks the monk-like look. But *lots* of guys look really sexy with a bald head."

My heart skipped a beat or two. Jeez, I was *not* comfortable with talking about sexy guys with him.

Denis grinned. "Yeah? Maybe I should go for the same solution, then? Just shave it all off before it falls out on its own?" He ran his hand through his hair again.

God, this conversation was stressing me out—but in the best kind of way.

"You'd totally rock the bald look," I told him. I held a finger up. "You'd have to be even more careful about going out in the sun, though!"

Denis threw back his head and laughed loud enough for Fidi and Tristan to look up from their computers on the other side of the room.

"If I ever do it," Denis said, laughing as he rolled his chair back to his own desk. "I'll make sure to buy sunblock at the same time."

"Make sure you do. I'll even help you rub it in, if you want."

The blush at having said that *out loud* stayed with me until five o'clock, when I could finally bail from the office to run home and hide in my pink blanket.

FIVE

Tea and a Pink Blanket

Ensconced in my chair with my pink blanket around me, I sipped at my herbal tea and clicked on the Refresh button on DD's author page every thirty seconds. I had an alert up for when she posted new stories, of course, but that could take up to five minutes before actually making my phone ping.

So I stayed with my trusted Refresh button.

I wondered what she had in store for Laure and Fred tonight.

In the last chapter they'd made out and gotten halfway to naked before being interrupted by the roommate. They'd gotten *caught* by the roommate, which I couldn't really remember happening in any other romances I'd read. Usually, they'd jump apart and look guilty, but basically have the time to get their clothes back on.

In DD's story, Laure and Fred had been on the couch, in plain view from the front door.

Fred, despite having his zipper open and hard dick clearly showing through his boxers, had been a perfect gentleman, and acted as a human shield for Laure while she got her bra and shirt back on.

Then the chapter ended.

Damn DD and her brilliant writing.

What was going to happen? Would Laure freak out at being caught? Would the roommate make fun of them? Would she still stay the night so I could get my super-hot sex scene?

I pressed Refresh again.

The new chapter appeared.

Yes!

Taking my first sip of my herbal tea and breaking into a huge smile, I started reading.

It continued from right after the last chapter! With the roommate sort of making fun of them, but in a supportive kind of way. He asked Fred if this was why he'd seemed so happy lately—because he was *in loooove*.

Aw, man. Yet another cliché. And yet another win from DD.

She was such a great storyteller.

Still no sex scene.

Laure went home and Fred stayed up late *talking about his feelings with his roommate*.

And I'd have to wait another week for the next chapter.

Lily: *You're killing me here, DD! When will I get my sex scene?*

DD: *I'm not telling! The anticipation is half the fun! That's how you build suspense in a romance—which I'm sure you know, having read all of your stories.*

Lily: *Not true! I tend to send them to bed really early in the story. I love it when there's lot of sexy times!*

DD: *As do I, Lily. But even if your hero and heroine sleep together early in the story, the suspense of when they will realize they're meant to be together remains. I happen to prefer for the feelz to be in place before they actually jump in the sack.*

Gulping down the rest of my now cold herbal tea, I pondered DD's words.

What she said was true, of course. I tended to have my two main characters lusting after each other—preferably despite hating each other—from the very start, and have some sort of catalyst—alcohol, upsetting life event, being forced to stay in a closed room together for a long period of time—shove them into their first sexual encounter. Then I'd work from there to get them to also fall in love with each other, realizing there's more than only the physical aspect of the other person that's attractive.

DD tended to do it the other way around. More of a friends-to-lovers kind of author.

I grunted and set my cup down on the floor before closing my blanket even tighter around myself and started typing.

Lily: *It's not really the case in my current story, though. Like I told you earlier, she already knows he's a really good guy on the inside, and now that he's cut his hair, she realizes he's also sexy. So the inside came before the outside!*

Hah. Take that, DD.

DD: *You're in chapter six, Lily. And I can feel the first sex scene coming, probably in one of next week's two chapters. So unless this is a novella and not a novel, they're going to jump in the sack in the first twenty percent of the story, without any* significant feelz in place, and we'll have lots of that awkward where-do-we-go-from-here that you're so good at.

She was right again.
Dammit.

A new message popped up, surprising me. Usually our messages would alternate, so we'd wait for the other to respond before sending another message.

DD: *Is that how you operate in real life, perhaps? Physical attraction first, then see if the feelz want to follow? I tried that route when I was younger, but got nothing but feeling hollow and lost from it, so I've decided not to sleep with anyone else unless I have real feelings for them. Guess that also translates into my writing.*

I frowned at the screen. Was she accusing me of sleeping around?

I chortled at the very idea.

Sleeping around is kind of difficult when you hardly ever even talk to guys in real life. I'd never had the guts to let a guy I liked know that I liked him. How embarrassing when he would turn me down!

I wasn't a complete innocent, or even a virgin, thank God. I had, somehow, happened upon a guy who was genuinely interested during a summer camp when I was eighteen, and we'd ended up sleeping together a total of three times before camp ended.

It had been sweet and fun and a promise of good things to come in the years ahead.

Except nobody else had ever shown any interest.

So I lived vicariously through stories—my own and those of other authors.

Lily: *You couldn't be further from the truth, DD. In real life, I wouldn't dream of sleeping with someone I didn't have feelings for. But stories are different, you know? There's no real risk.*

I guess I let my characters take the risks I'm not willing to take myself. Probably because I'm the author, so I know the feelings will come along eventually and it will all be worth it in the end.

Real life doesn't have those kinds of guarantees.

DD: *True, dat. But I've always wondered: does that make real life worse? Or does it mean that it will be even* more *satisfying if you* do *end up with the feelz?*

SIX

High on Yoga and Endorphins

It was ten o'clock on a Sunday morning and I was about to have my weekly dose of socializing.

Somehow, miraculously, I'd managed to keep in touch with my three best friends from high school. We'd been an inseparable, geeky group back then, had been split up by two of us studying in different cities for five years, then managed to all find jobs back in Toulouse once we had our diplomas in hand.

We no longer lived in the same part of town, though, so at first we'd had trouble actually meeting up, doing the whole "we really need to catch up soon" every week or two.

Chloé, the loudest of the group—although that doesn't mean all that much in a group of horribly shy girls—finally had enough and forced a meet-up in a café in the city center. Then she declared that the situation was unacceptable and we needed to set up a regular time and place to meet or we'd all lose each other's friendship.

The discussion on when and where to meet took forever. We proposed cafés, restaurants, bowling sessions, hiking…but it was impossible to find something that everybody liked.

Finally, when we were all about to give up, Sabrina said, "I recently paid for a yearly subscription to a yoga app. It's quite fun, even alone. We could do an hour of yoga together? And perhaps have lunch afterward?"

Silence.

Her straight, jaw-length black hair framed her pretty face, as usual, but as the silence stretched, she tilted her head forward a fraction, so the bangs would fall almost into her eyes and the hair on the sides covered more of her reddening cheeks.

"You do yoga?" I asked.

She shrugged and looked down at her hands. "Did a few classes at uni. Makes me feel all relaxed after." Her gaze darted around to meet our eyes. "Didn't feel like going to a class here, since I wouldn't know anyone."

"I wouldn't mind feeling relaxed," Chloé said. "And it might be fun to do it together."

So we tried it.

And never looked back.

Sabrina was right—yoga does make you all relaxed. And also? It's a shit-load of fun when you do it with your best friends.

So here we were, in Sabrina's living room—because she was the only one in the group to have a room big enough to house a four-person yoga class—trying to decide if we wanted an all-around work-out or if we wanted a special focus on the "core."

"I'm not sure if my core is up to a focused work-out today," Caroline said. "It's still busy digesting the three *chocolatines* I had for breakfast."

"You had *three*?" Sabrina's tone was a mix of disbelief, disappointment, and mirth.

Caroline had always had trouble limiting herself when it came to sweets, and living alone and being responsible for what ended up on her plate hadn't helped things. She wasn't quite fat, I wouldn't go that far, but she needed to watch out if she didn't want to end up there.

"Core it is," I said, clapping my hands together. I pointed at Caroline and lifted an eyebrow. "Those *chocolatines* are going to be history."

Caroline rolled her eyes at me, grinning. "Fine." She settled onto her mat. "Means there will be more room for lunch. Ha!"

Chuckling at our friend, we all took our places and Sabrina pressed start on the app.

"So, how's the writing going?" Chloé asked as she relaxed into Child pose.

I smiled into my mat. "Great. Still managing to get up two chapters a week."

"And when are we going to get to read it?"

Every week, we had this same discussion.

"Never. When are you going to stop harassing me?"

Chloé chuckled as she pushed up into Tabletop. "Never."

"I need to be confident that nobody I actually know in real life will ever read what I write," I told her for the hundredth time. "Otherwise, I'd picture everyone reading what I write and I just *know* it would stop me from writing freely."

"But we already know you write porn," Caroline said.

We all giggled at the ongoing joke between us, but mine turned into a groan as I stretched my back into Cow pose. "It's romance. Not porn." I added under my breath, "And this is why I'll never tell you how to find my stories."

"I'd give you so many likes." Caroline smiled at me as she stretched, showing off how nimble she was despite her size. "I'd give you so many comments."

"I prefer the real comments," I told her. "From the people who do it because they like the story, not because they like me."

"So that DD chick who keeps your nose in your phone twenty-four seven," Chloé said. "She only likes you for your stories?"

I sent my friend an angry stare. "Of course not! We're friends now. But, yes, it started out with a mutual admiration for each other's stories."

We were up to the more active part of the yoga session, with Sun Salutations, so we talked less as we concentrated on the positions.

Well, most of us talked less. Chloé, who was a work-out fanatic, had no trouble to keep talking.

"If she wasn't a chick," she said, "I'd be worried about you getting so hung up on someone you met on the internet. I know we're the generation who lives on the internet and everything, but it opens up for the creeps to do so much potential damage."

"DD isn't a creep," I told her as my right leg started cramping for staying in Warrior Two for too long. "She's my friend."

"Leave her alone," Sabrina said, always the peace-maker. "She's allowed to have friends outside of our group and is a big girl who can take care of herself."

"Thank you," I told Sabrina with a smile.

"Welcome! Now, tell me, how are things going with Denis?"

I groaned, and not because of the stretch we were apparently supposed to hold for thirty seconds. "Really, Sabrina? I thought you were the nice one."

"I am!" Her smile took over her entire face, making her almond-shaped eyes turn into slits.

She had such a beautiful face. It should be a crime that she felt the need to hide it behind her hair all the time.

"I am a nice friend who cares about you and know that you'd love to talk to us about your crush."

I felt myself blushing but hoped it would be hidden by my tomato-red work-out face. "It's not a crush."

"Yes, it is," Caroline singsonged.

"When can we meet him?" Chloé asked.

Yeah, right. "Never. I do not trust you people."

"But we're your friends!" Caroline was enjoying this way too much.

Must find a way to pay her back.

"And you're great friends," I told them—because they were. "But there's no way in hell I'm introducing you to Denis. Or anyone else at work, for that matter."

"Aww." Chloé put a hand to her heart in mock hurt, breaking out of the Relaxed Warrior stance. "Are you ashamed of us?"

"Yes," I deadpanned. A brief pause. "But I love you guys anyway."

An hour later, we were all showered and relaxed as usual, in line to buy salads and sandwiches at the closest *boulangerie*.

"I'm totally getting the American again," Caroline said, her eyes hungrily scanning the menu.

"Oh, please don't," Chloé said. "I can't stand to see a *sandwich* filled with *two* chopped steaks *and* fries. I'm going to explode just watching you."

Caroline sighed but her sigh was quickly followed by a chuckle. "You're such a drama queen. Fine, I'll have the Mediterranean."

Which meant it'd be soaked in olive oil. But at least it was vegetables and a lot better than the American.

We did this every week. It was only one meal out of God knows how many in her week, and Caroline knew what we were doing, but it was our way of showing her that we cared. We knew she wanted to eat better and to lose a couple of kilos, but we also knew she wasn't in the right place in her head right now. She needed comfort food.

Except when she was with us.

Or at least, that's what we'd decided.

We found a table by the window, giving us a great view over Toulouse. Sabrina lived at Jolimont, one of two hills in an otherwise completely flat city, and this *boulangerie* stood at the top of the main road leading to the top, allowing us to spot the spires of at least one cathedral, one basilica, and one desacralized church.

One of these days, I might even go so far as to go inside one of them to have a look around.

Or not.

I sat down, my body energized and relaxed all at once. My legs felt like they'd be able to run a marathon, my arms like they actually had muscles, and my abs like they'd be flat for at least one day. My head was at ease and I knew I sported the same goofy grin as my friends.

"So, Laure," Chloé said, as I bit into my spicy chicken sandwich. "How was Denis this week?"

I leaned back in my seat, a grin spreading across my face. "Dreamy."

Caroline giggled. "I don't know why we bother asking her anything before the yoga. Everything is so much easier after."

Chloé gave her a mock glare. "Because she needs to be able to tell us this stuff even when she's not high on yoga and endorphins."

Caroline shrugged, already halfway through her sandwich.

In a deceptively calm voice, Sabrina asked, "What's your author name?"

I touched my barrette, and the white lily it held. I took it off for yoga, but always put it back on before going out to eat. I felt naked without it.

"Not telling," I told her, a serene smile on my face.

"Mmm," Chloé said around a mouthful of salad. "I think we might need to mix yoga and alcohol for her to answer that one."

Caroline lit up. "We should totally do yoga and alcohol!"

Groans and laughter all around.

"So have you talked to him yet?" Chloé asked.

"Yes," I replied, not meeting her eyes.

"About something else than work."

I ground my teeth together, totally behaving like a stubborn five-year-old. Then I lit up. "Yes! We talked about hair."

"Hair." Caroline's voice was completely flat. "I thought you said he didn't have much of it."

"He doesn't. But I kind of…" I drifted off as I wondered how this would sound. "I told him his brother would look sexy if he shaved his head?"

Caroline almost choked on her sandwich and Sabrina had apple juice spurting out of her nose.

"You told him what, now?" Chloé asked.

"It totally made sense in context! He said his brother had been bald for ages, but let the hair grow where he still had some and I told him he'd probably be better off to just shave everything off."

I was met with three doubtful looks.

"You have the weirdest flirting game ever," Caroline finally said.

"I wasn't flirting!"

"Well," Chloé said with finality in her tone. "You really should."

Totally never happening.

SEVEN

We Only Talked about It Once

For once, I was the first to arrive in the office. The blinds were down, the lights off, and the air conditioning on. Fidi was usually the last one to leave in the evening and his explanation for always leaving the air conditioning on was that in the Albi offices it was all automated.

Or, possibly, he had other things on his mind when he left at who knows what hour at night.

I flipped the light switch as I passed the door and set my purse on my desk before moving over to roll open the two right-hand blinds. The one on the left had apparently been stuck for a year and a half and nobody had any faith it would ever be fixed.

Outside, the sky was as perfect and blue as it had been two minutes ago when I got out of my car but it was somehow even worse now that I was stuck in the office.

I opened the window, hoping to get some spring air.

Which meant I needed to turn off the air conditioning.

I stalked over to the small console by the door, trying—not for the first time—to make sense of the thing. There were numbers and there were signs of a snowflake, a sun, and a fan. Did sun mean air conditioning or heat? Did I really need to know to turn the damn thing off? And those numbers on top. It was always a number but never the same—

"It's the day of the week!" I exclaimed to myself. Which was totally useless to me right now.

In the end, I went with my usual solution to problems with buttons. I pressed everything until it seemed to be off.

"There we go," I told myself with a wide grin.

The door flew open, barely missing my nose.

"Denis!" My heart hammered in my chest and I put a hand to my heart like some sort of swooning lady. "You scared the *hell* out of me."

"I'm so sorry!" His eyes went wide and his mouth hung open as he looked me over, probably looking for an injury.

I'd never seen his eyes look quite that big before.

Then I realized why that was and I couldn't hold back my gasp.

"You cut your hair!"

Self-consciously, he ran his hand over his newly shorn head. "Yeah…"

"But… But…" I raged an inner battle with myself, fighting the words that wanted to come out from leaving my mouth.

But I told him *his brother* should cut his hair.

We only talked about it *once*.

He totally *rocked* the look.

I needed to say something, and soon, or I'd have to ask to change projects so I'd never have to come face to face with him again.

But he was so *hot*.

My silence made Denis talkative. He tended to do that when a silence went on too long. He filled the space.

"I was going to cut it this weekend anyway. And then after our conversation, I wondered if perhaps I should just cut it all off. It'd definitely be easier, you know? And I could save a buck or two if I use my electric razor. Not that I had the guts to do it myself the first time. So I went to my appointment at the hairdresser and asked her opinion. She thought I should go for it. So I did."

Silence descended again and we were both blushing.

Denis chuckled awkwardly. "I can get up at least ninety seconds later in the morning now, since I don't have to worry about doing my hair."

Finally, I broke out of my spell.

"Ninety seconds, huh? Sounds like your hair really was a priority." I adjusted my barrette. I'd gone with a red flower that didn't pretend to be anything specific but was still pretty, because it went with my red blouse.

A genuine smile stretched across Denis' face as his hand ran over his non-existent hair again. "I did consider getting a comb-over, but figured it would be too much work."

My hand flew to my mouth as I giggled.

I realized we were just standing there, in the office doorway, so I walked over to my seat, and Denis trailed after me.

"So it doesn't look *too* bad?" Denis asked as he removed his jacket. "You think the guys will make fun of me?"

"I certainly hope not," I said, outraged at the idea. "And it looks great."

Of course, my cheeks flamed again but I was in luck because Denis had his back turned while he settled in at his own desk.

I couldn't stop staring.

It was like my own story was coming to life in front of my eyes. I had totally projected myself into the main character of the story, and Denis as the romantic interest. My character had been sort of attracted to the guy in the beginning, and then when he shaved his head, *boom!* He was irresistible.

And she jumped him. First sex scene, six chapters in.

So, yeah. Any comparison to my own life ended here.

Still. I had to remind myself I'd been attracted to Denis before he cut all his hair off and became all sexy and stuff—which was really stupid, seeing how I'd spent hours of my Sunday trying, and failing, to resist gushing over him to my friends.

Totally never telling them.

Fidi barged through the door, his jacket already halfway off and the backpack with his laptop open. The guy was usually working before he was even in his seat. I wasn't sure what the urgency was about, but as long as nobody told me, there was nothing I could do about it.

He took the time to come over and do *la bise* in greeting, and he shook Denis' hand. "Hey, nice haircut," he said. "Suits you. Sexy."

And he was back at his desk, tapping along at his keyboard.

Denis, poor guy, was left with his hand still outstretched and a healthy blush on his cheeks.

I was about to say something to get Denis to snap out of whatever was going on in his head when Tristan walked through the door.

He grabbed Denis' outstretched hand as if he was used to his colleagues sitting around waiting for the opportunity to shake his hand. "Morning."

He greeted me, then went over to shake Fidi's hand and completely forgot they weren't the only two in the room. I could have danced a jig and they wouldn't have noticed.

I'd say I'd never met such workaholics before, but since this is my very first job, that doesn't carry as much punch as I'd have liked.

"See," I told Denis. "He didn't even see the hair. Or rather, the lack of hair."

Denis huffed a laugh. "I guess you're right."

But I could tell he kept an eye on Fidi for the rest of the day, which was all types of hilarious.

EIGHT

You Had Lots of Sex?

Lily: *Something totally weird happened today. This guy that I work with, who may or may not have been the inspiration for the romantic interest in my current story, SHAVED HIS HEAD!*

DD: *So…if we go by your storyline, you had lots of sex? I do hope you did it at home and not at work, because I'm pretty sure that's frowned upon.*

Lily: *Ha, ha, bloody ha! I told him it looked good, though.*

DD: *Good for you. On a scale from dainty spring flower to deathly hemorrhage, how hard did you blush?*

Lily: *It's scary how well you know me, DD.*

Lily: Probably open flesh wound. But I don't think he saw!

DD: So you based your character on a guy you have a crush on, huh?

Lily: Like you've never done it.

DD: Oh, I've totally done it. What's the point in writing romance if you don't have a crush on your characters?

Lily: So is Fred from your current story based on someone real?

DD: Wouldn't you like to know.

Lily: Yes, I would! Come on, don't make me feel all stalkery and alone, here. Please tell me you also live vicariously through your stories.

DD: Fine. Yes, my character is based on my current crush.

Lily: Victory!!! Makes me wonder where you work, though. Fred is a total hunk with a mountain of muscles. Ain't none of that where I work…

NINE

I Must Be Hallucinating

The team was going on a trip. Suddenly, out of nowhere, it was apparently essential that we have a team-building weekend and it needed to be *this* weekend.

Not that I minded. A free trip to the Pyrenees, all expenses paid?

I'm in!

I told the girls I wouldn't be able to make it to Sunday yoga and after the story checked out they all declared we could still all be friends.

I spent at least an hour on Thursday night trying to decide if I should bring my laptop or not. Going a whole weekend without it felt *wrong* somehow, and I thought it was a very real possibility that I'd suffer from withdrawal symptoms if I couldn't spend hours on the writing forum like I usually did.

In the end, I managed to leave it behind—carefully hidden at the back of my closet so potential thieves wouldn't find it too easily—but only because I knew I could do pretty much everything except writing a new chapter on my phone.

I could read DD's upcoming chapter on Saturday.

I could read and write comments on stories.

I could keep chatting with my online friend.

So I showed up to work on Friday morning with a backpack that was lighter than I'd ever felt it because it *didn't* contain a laptop, but feeling pretty good about myself for doing the adult thing.

Both Fidi and Tristan were in the office before me when I arrived, both so immersed in their work I had to tap them on the shoulder for them to notice me and say hello.

As I waited for my work laptop to boot, I tapped in a message to DD on my phone. I had to make absolutely sure I'd be able to keep contact this weekend—otherwise I was totally going home during lunch break to get my personal laptop.

> **Lily:** *I'm going on a trip with my team at work this weekend. Just wanted to give you a heads up that I'll probably be a little less wordy than usual and might not always have coverage. *shudders**

I tapped in my login and password on my work laptop, then turned toward the door in time to see Denis walk in with his nose in his phone. He wore a goofy smile and his eyes crinkled.

How I wished I was the one to make him smile like that.

He shook hands with Fidi and Tristan, not having much more luck than me with tearing them away from whatever they were working on together, then dumped his phone, jacket and sports bag on his seat before greeting me.

"All ready and packed, I see?" He nodded toward my backpack. "Whose car are you riding in?"

"No idea," I told him, my eyes wide. "Is that supposed to already be decided?" I hoped I wouldn't be left behind because nobody thought to save me a spot.

"Don't worry about it," Denis said, his smile even wider than when he entered and his eyes warm. He turned to Tristan. "Hey, *chef*!" he yelled to get the other guy to react. "There's room for Laure in your car, isn't there?"

Tristan looked away from Fidi for long enough to answer, "Sure. No problem."

"See?" Denis tapped a staccato rhythm on his desk as he swung his chair to face his desk, settling in. "The four of us will share a car."

A huge grin spread across my face at the idea of sharing a car with Denis for over an hour.

Luckily, Denis didn't see it because once he'd tapped in his login and password, his nose was back in his phone as he tapped a message.

I returned to my own laptop, which was finally ready for me. I opened my emails, Eclipse and the Scrum tool that would tell me what bug I needed to work on today.

I heard Denis sigh as he put down his phone. "Here we go," he mumbled as he opened his emails.

My phone vibrated.

> **DD**: *No worries! Believe it or not, I'm also going away this weekend, also to a spot that's bound to have bad coverage. I'm going hiking! Don't worry, though. My next chapter is ready to go live on Saturday without me. I'll be reading the comments!*

I sat there staring at my phone for several minutes.

This couldn't be possible.

I re-read the message four more times, every time remembering the timing of events since Denis came through the door.

No way.

DD was *a girl*.

A girl who wrote romance, for crying out loud.

I must be hallucinating.

Still.

Lily: *Don't fall off a cliff or anything! I need you to finish the story, not just the next chapter!*

I hit send.

Five seconds.

Denis' phone whistled with an incoming message.

TEN

How?!?

No way.
 No.
 Not possible.
 How?!?
 Denis picked up his phone, read the message and smiled. Started typing in a response.
 Panic rising, I fumbled with my phone, trying to remember how to turn off the vibrations. Mine doesn't ping when I get a message, but it does vibrate.
 Denis put his phone back on the desk next to his keyboard.
 My phone vibrated before I could turn the feature off but since I was holding it in my hand, Denis didn't notice.
 I let out a breath. Slowly.

Looked down at my phone.

DD: *I'm afraid I've only set up this next chapter for an automatic upload. But don't worry—I won't fall off the mountain! I might not be what you'd call an athlete, but I can manage to keep on my feet.*

Shit. Denis was DD.
DD was Denis.
HOW??!?

ELEVEN

I Had Info

THAT FRIDAY WAS not my most efficient.

I looked at the bug I was supposed to correct today, not really making any sense of it. I opened the relevant bit of code on one screen.

Then on my second screen, the one that was turned away from Denis on my right—and I turned it away a little farther to be safe—I opened the writing forum.

I'd hardly ever done this at work before. I knew I shouldn't do it now. But I couldn't wait *three whole days* before looking into it.

So I tried—and failed miserably, but nobody caught me at it—to multitask.

I opened the chat I had going with DD. Three hundred and twenty-six messages total.

How had I not realized DD was a guy?

So I went through them all, looking for clues.

Fist finding: he'd never actually used the words "her," "she," or "girlfriend." The sentences were all turned in such a way that it could be either. And since I'd assumed from the start that DD was girl—guys aren't supposed to write romance!—my brain had interpreted everything the way I wanted to see it.

A little more reassuring was my second finding: *I* hadn't been vague. I'd asked about boyfriends, how he/she felt about certain male characters' looks, if he/she—jeez, I still couldn't quite merge DD and Denis into one person in my head—would be attracted to a certain type of guy.

The answers were, of course, kind of vague. Keeping in mind that DD was in fact a straight guy, I could now see how he skirted the issue. Answered the more direct questions in a way that *could* be a guy saying, "Sure, he's attractive if you're into that kind of thing."

Which he wasn't.

The more indirect questions, he answered more in detail and with honesty. At least, I supposed so. If I asked him how he'd felt about a particular scene, he told me what he liked, what he didn't. What turned him on, what made him put the story down in disgust.

Aaaargh.

I had info on what turned Denis on in a story.

My eyes actually scanned past those messages, too weirded out by my new discovery and the fact that he was sitting less than two meters away.

I'd get back to them, though.

Just not right now.

Then I reached our most recent exchanges. The ones about his work in progress.

Where the heroine is named Laure.

And I got stuck on the message where he said his character was based on his crush.

I'd assumed he talked about Fred, since I'd assumed DD was a girl. A straight girl. But DD was a guy. Who was attracted to girls.

Which meant his crush was reflected in the *female* character.

Who was named Laure.

Like me.

"Are you getting anywhere with that bug?" Denis' face was suddenly *right there*, approaching my screen to see what had me so engrossed.

With a shriek, I panicked and pressed the Windows and L keys to lock my computer.

"I was just going to the bathroom!" I said too loudly, making even Tristan and Fidi look up from what they were doing.

Eyes wide and mouth hanging open, Denis had one hand suspended over my desk where he was about to set it down.

"Sorry," I said as I pushed my chair away from my desk. "I was in the zone and was about to go to the toilet and you scared me."

At least some of that was true.

Trying for dignity but probably failing miserably, I fled the office.

After a pep-talk in front of the mirror, I returned to the office and managed to meet Denis' is-the-woman-going-to-blow-up-in-our-faces look with a smile.

"Sorry, again," I said with a chuckle. "You really did give me a scare. I'd love some help with that bug now." I logged in, minimized the browser open to our online conversations, then closed it.

I was never opening that in the office ever again. I was too young to die of a heart attack.

Expression back to his sweet normal, Denis scooted his chair over. "Wow, you really are stuck, huh?"

I hadn't written a single line of code since that morning. "I'm a little preoccupied with something personal today," I explained, my face heating. "I'm sure I could figure out how to fix this myself, but I'm not actually sure I've understood what the problem is in the first place."

"No worries," Denis said. He hovered his hand over mine on the mouse. "Can I?"

The heat of his hand, even if there was no actual contact, made a jolt of electricity shoot up my arm and I pulled my hand away at lightning speed.

Denis went through the description of the bug with me and made sure I understood the problem. Chances were, I would have been stuck on this one even if my mind hadn't been elsewhere because there was one principle that I simply hadn't known. Denis did, and explained it to me in a way that made it interesting and without making me feel like an idiot.

"They don't teach that in school," he said, shaking his head. "But it keeps popping up in real life. Won't be the first time you see it."

"Thank you, Denis," I said, daring meeting his gaze for the first time since my revelation. Only for a second or two, though.

His smile was seriously brighter than the sun, and that damned bald head of his made his beautiful brown eyes stand out.

"My pleasure," he replied as he scooted back to his place. "And, you know, just doing my job."

Denis was our team's Tech Lead, which meant that he was supposed to field all technical questions. "I don't see the others asking you questions about their bugs," I grumbled.

He shrugged. "They should. Asking questions is a good thing."

"There's no such thing as a stupid question?"

He barked a laugh. "Oh, there's such a thing as a stupid question. But you haven't asked any stupid questions yet."

Not quite knowing what to do with the happiness warming me from the inside out, I turned back to my computer and vowed to get this bloody bug fixed before the day was over.

TWELVE

So Much More Perfect Than Me

I FIXED THE bug. And I spent about an hour reading the same sentence over and over—on my phone so I couldn't be caught in the act.

Yes, my character is based on my current crush.

He was either gay and had a crush on our colleague Olivier, who was the only one with enough muscles to be anywhere near the description of Fred, the romantic interest, or he had a crush on a girl who'd inspired the character who shared a name with me.

Could I really be Denis' crush?

The very idea flooded me with so many emotions all at once, I had no idea where to start or what to feel.

Someone had a crush on me, which had, as far as I knew, never happened before. That someone was none other than the guy *I* was currently crushing on.

He'd made the story version of me so much more perfect than me. She had better hair, a prettier nose, livelier eyes. She was super smart and sweetly funny. I didn't like that he'd needed to improve me like that in order to be able to sell me as a lovable character for his story.

Which reminded me that I'd also based my current romantic interest on him. What if *he* made the same connection I made and realized I had a crush on him? I'd die of embarrassment.

Denis—who was most undeniably a guy—*wrote romance*. I'd pictured him in his free time doing manly things like…like… which was when I realized that I hadn't the slightest idea what his hobbies were, what he spent his free time on.

How was it possible that I'd crushed on the guy for months and never wondered what he did outside of office hours?

Oh, right, by being super shy and hardly ever being the one to initiate a conversation with the guy.

But…*romance*?

Okay, I was totally judging a guy for having the same interests as me, a girl. I was sure there was something wrong with that. If girls were allowed to do stuff like racing cars and play rugby, then guys should be allowed to read and write love stories.

Right?

Suppressing a groan, I closed my phone to stop seeing that damned sentence—*yes, my character is based on my current crush*—and shut down my laptop.

It was six o'clock and we were leaving for our weekend in the Pyrenees.

I was going to spend the next hour in a car with Denis.

My phone vibrated with a new message. My heart sped into overdrive.

THIRTEEN

007 Does Romance

DD: *I started reading a new book last night. Decided to try out a hockey romance instead of my usual football ones. So far it seems really promising!*

I read the message as I followed the rest of the team out to the parking lot. Denis was right in front of me and kept glancing at his phone in his hand, clearly waiting for an answer.

I had no idea what to write.

I needed help. I opened the group chat with the girls and typed as quickly as I could.

Laure: *Help! Discovered that my online friend DD is actually Denis from my team. What do I do?!?*

Chloé: *The online friend who writes romance?!? No way!*

Laure: *Yes way. Now I know who he is but he doesn't know I'm me. He sent me a message on the forum and I HAVE NO IDEA HOW TO RESPOND.*

Sabrina: *No need for all caps. Just answer like you normally would.*

Chloé: *This is the perfect opportunity to get information on the guy you like!*

Sabrina: *You should tell him about it. Keeping secrets like that is never a good idea.*

I glanced up from my phone at Denis. He stood leaning against Tristan's car, his phone still in his hand. Both our bags were in Tristan's trunk and we were waiting for the rest of the team to figure out who went in which car.

I tried imagining going up to him and saying, "Hey, guess what? I'm Lily from the writers' forum."

So not happening.

I was blushing at the mere idea.

I had shared a lot of private details of my life with DD. Talked about my feelings, my insecurities. I shared things that you're supposed to share with your friends—I shared even more than with the girls on certain subjects because I had the safety of anonymity.

No way in hell was I giving up my anonymity.

Laure: *Sorry, Sabrina. That's never going to happen.*

Chloé: *Because you're going to take this opportunity to find out about the guy you like! You should ask him what he likes and use that to seduce him!*

Laure: *I think you forget who you're talking to. I've never seduced anyone in my life. I wouldn't know how to go about it. And would likely die of a heart attack if I ever tried!*

Chloé: *Nonsense. You've been scared in the past because you're afraid of rejection. Now you can test the waters risk-free!*

Sabrina: *That is such a bad idea. Tell him who you are, Laure.*

Chloé: *You already know lots of stuff about him but I'm sure you can get more! Ask him what hobbies he likes. What sports. What types of movies. If he says he's dying to see the next Avengers movie, tell him in passing one day when you're going to see it. I guarantee he'll tag along!*

My heart hammered in my chest at the mere idea of doing what Chloé suggested. But the concept also had some merit.

The entire team was ready for departure. Denis got into the backseat of Tristan's car. Fidi was some distance off, talking to Mathieu, so I had the choice between riding up front with Tristan and the back with Denis.

Should have been a no-brainer, but all of a sudden I was terrified that Denis would discover my online persona simply by being near me.

So I just stood there, unable to decide.

Sitting with the boss, risking one hour of awkward silence or talking work on a Friday night.

Or sitting next to my crush, who was also my online friend, and who had the power to humiliate me if he put two and two together.

Fidi ended up deciding for me. He walked up, saw me standing closer to the backseat than the front, asked, "You're getting in the back? Guess I'll sit with the boss, then," and took the front seat.

Without meeting Denis' gaze, I got into the backseat.

He still had his phone in his hand but he was still waiting for a reply, so he turned to me with a hesitant smile, clearly thinking he'd need to make small talk.

Lily: *Yeah? What's the book? Tell me all about it.*

The distraction worked.

Denis' phone whistled an incoming message and he bent his head over his phone to read it. He started typing a reply immediately.

I went back to messaging with my friends.

Laure: *I don't think I can do that. I'm freaking out just being in the same car as him right now. I don't think my voice would work if I tried talking to him.*

Chloé: *Then do the online part first! Get the info you need to seduce him. Eventually, you'll get used to the idea and you'll be able to talk to him in person again. Right now it's all fresh! First things first: intel.*

Laure: *I don't even know where to start.*

My phone vibrated with an incoming message from the writers' forum. Almost dropping my phone in my haste, I turned off the vibration mode on my phone. Denis shouldn't have been able to hear when it vibrated in my hand, but I wasn't taking any chances.

DD: *Here's the link to the author website. She seems to have been around a while, judging by the number of titles. I'm on my first one, where the guy is a professional hockey player and the woman is some old flame who suddenly works for his team. The writing is awesome and the characters feel real, you* know? I have a feeling I'll be reading all of her books over the next weeks.

Lily: *Sounds great. I'll check it out. So you're continuing on the theme of hunks with muscles, huh?*

As I pressed send, I felt my face flame with embarrassment. I was talking about hunks with muscles with a *guy*. A straight guy. Who I had a crush on. I turned my face toward the window, pretending to be absolutely fascinated by the passing houses and roundabouts.

Laure: *I can't do this, Chloé. I asked a question, but I'm so embarrassed right now I'm probably heating the car with my cheeks alone.*

Sabrina: *Don't follow Chloé's stupid plan. Wait until you're alone with him and tell him. Or write it on that forum of yours.*

Chloé: *You'll get used to it! Take it one question at a time. If you're in a car together, watch how he reacts to your messages. Watch his face when he's typing the reply. Seriously, this is the perfect opportunity to get to know the guy and give yourself the confidence to talk to him about something other than work in real life.*

Logically, I *knew* that Sabrina was right. Going through with Chloé's weird 007-does-romance plan would not end well.

But coming clean with Denis just wasn't possible.

I'd been shy my entire life, so I knew how this worked. Sometimes, I'd need to talk to someone but really didn't want to, and I'd need to work up to it. Had to convince myself that I had no choice. That if I didn't, it would have a bad outcome. Like not graduating, or not keeping my job. Not *getting* the job.

Then I'd force the first words out. The first were always the most difficult.

Because as long as I hadn't started, I could still change my mind.

Once the first words were out, the risk of stopping was greater. Saying three words and then stopping? That would bring even more embarrassment.

So once I got started, the rest of the sentence would follow.

Not gracefully. My voice would often waver and I'd not look the person in the eyes.

But I said whatever it was I needed to say.

Right now, with Denis, I didn't *have to* talk to him. There was no immediate or direct backlash if I didn't.

Sure, it had a potential gain—if he *did* have a crush on me, this could be awesome—but it wasn't enough to make up for the risks.

What if he *didn't* like me that way?

What if he got mad when he realized I knew he read and wrote romance?

What if he told the rest of the team that *I* wrote romance? I wasn't embarrassed about it *per se*, but explaining romance to people who had never read it was…tiring. They judged the book by its cover—preferably the ones from the eighties with half-naked women on them—and would never consider even giving it a chance.

When I met other people who read the same types of books, I had no trouble gushing over my passion for them. But not to just anyone.

And not at work.

Denis was still typing his answer. From time to time, he took a break and stared unseeingly out the window.

What was he so pensive about?

Guess I'd find out once he sent his reply.

Laure: *Okay, Chloé, I see your point. Not sure if I can really do it, especially on the types of subjects you're thinking about, but I'll give it a shot.*

Sabrina: *This isn't going to end well.*

She was probably right.
A new message popped up on the writers' forum.

FOURTEEN

Men with Muscles!

DD: *The muscles aren't the important bit, you know. I don't know why I tend to like romances in the sports world, I just do. It's not because of the muscles, though, I know that much.*

I guess there's something vibrant about the characters, and not just the athletes. Is it possible the fact that they do sports and have a very active life sort of bleeds over into the story?

Or perhaps I simply need to read something that's far from my own everyday life. Professional sports is definitely that.

Lily: *What is your day job, anyway? I don't think you ever said.*

DD: *It's a nine-to-five office job. I quite like it, but it's not exactly a passionate subject to discuss with someone who's not a computer geek.*

Lily: *Well, you can discuss it with me, if you like. I'm a computer geek, too!*

DD: *Sure took you long to write such a short reply. Not sure if you wanted to share? I don't blame you. But knowing you're a computer geek is hardly enough to find you on Google.*

Lily: *I'll have you know I was interrupted, which is why the reply took so long. Told you I was going away this weekend, remember?*

DD: *Right. For someone who's supposed to be socializing, you are spending a lot of time on your phone. Not that I mind!*

Lily: *Hey, I checked out the website of that author. She does have a lot of books out. I think I'll try one of them out. Which one do you think I should start with?*

DD: *Why don't you start on the one I'm reading? That way we can discuss along the way. Here's the link.*

Lily: *Hey, I see she also has some M/M books. That's kind of original.*

DD: *Yeah, I saw those. Not sure if those are for me, though. I'll let you try them out first!*

Lily: *Not for you? It's romance. Men with muscles! Twice as much muscles as usual!*

DD: *There's more to romance than muscles.*

FIFTEEN

Good Little Geeks

As our chat progressed, I leaned halfway against the car door, so I could survey Denis out of the corner of my eye.

He was smiling throughout, which helped tremendously with my nerves. I could tease him a little, check that he wasn't insulted, then crank it up a notch.

The only time his smile faltered was at the mention of a double set of muscles.

Would that have made me wonder if DD was a man or a woman if we'd had that discussion a week ago? Would I have found it weird that a girl wouldn't want to read a story about two men falling in love?

Probably not.

There *were* women who read only love stories between men and women.

Apparently.

I was completely sold on the concept myself. Not to the point of reading only M/M stories—why would I deprive myself of so many wonderful M/F stories?—but enough that when I found a new writer who wrote both, I'd start with the ones with an all-male cast.

I didn't really understand *why* I loved those stories so much.

I mean, sure, it's two great and lovable guys, so I could fall for the both of them. But that wasn't all.

My current theory was that when the story was between two guys, there wasn't one who was "the strong one" and one who was "the weak one who has to be rescued." No, all female protagonists weren't weak. But… It was definitely the guy who was the protector, the strong one. If the female character was too strong, we moved into bitch territory real quick.

When it was two guys, they *had* to show emotions. They had to be the one to be rescued—might be both of them at different times in the story!—and the one to melt or swoon.

It made them more approachable.

More real.

I started my foray into M/M romance the same way I started on M/F: Harry Potter fanfiction.

See, at some point, I had basically read all the Harry/Ginny and Ron/Hermione fanfiction that was out there—all the good ones anyway—so I checked out the other pairings.

At first I was shocked—and I mean *shocked*—to discover that the most popular pairing of all was Harry/Draco.

They were two guys! They were sworn enemies!

At which point I went, "Ooooh! Enemies to lovers!"

And I tried one of the stories.

Almost failed biology my senior year of high school, but it was totally worth it.

It wasn't something I talked about, though. Not even on the writers' forum, mostly because I hadn't seen any M/M stories from my writer friends.

I was too shy to talk about that subject at all, even online.

So why was I bringing it up *now*? Now that I knew that DD was a guy? A colleague?

I might have lost my mind a little bit.

Or, my mind offered helpfully, I was making absolutely sure that I wouldn't be telling Denis the truth anytime soon. If I told him too many things that I didn't want him to know *officially*, I would never be able to come clean, and I could stay in my safe anonymity.

Denis lowered his phone to his lap after sending that last message instead of holding it up and waiting for my reply like he'd done up until now. He leaned his head against the window and gazed out at the approaching Pyrenees, fabulously beautiful against a darkening blue sky.

A small frown marked his forehead.

Maybe being honest would be a good thing in this situation.

Starting to type before I could change my mind, I wrote my longest message to DD ever, explaining my theories about M/M romance and why it appealed to me so much.

My last paragraph before hitting send:

Lily: *Romance has nothing to do with muscles and everything to do with what makes a person who he or she is on the inside. The wrapping on a gift might make you want to open it because it's all pretty and shiny, but if whatever you find on the inside is garbage, the paper gets thrown out with the rest.*

When Denis' phone whistled the arrival of my message, he didn't open it straight away. He flipped the phone over twice, as if he wasn't sure he wanted to read it.

He glanced my way, but I was ready for it and had my nose in my phone, only watching him in my peripheral vision.

Once he started reading, I stared outright.

He took his sweet time reading. His expression didn't change; he stayed pensive and serious. But I could literally see the tension leaking out of him the further along he read.

The last part even earned me a tiny smile.

He looked up then, and caught me staring at him.

Inside, I panicked, but somehow, miraculously, I stayed calm and kept the blushing to a minimum.

I held up my phone. "Guess we're being good little geeks with our noses in our phones instead of socializing, huh?"

This earned me an even bigger smile and I did an internal happy dance.

"Yeah, that wasn't really the point of this weekend, was it?" Denis looked to the front of the car to see if Fidi or Tristan heard us, but those two had been talking films and gaming since before we left the parking lot at work, oblivious to anything going on in the backseat.

"Well, I had some stuff I had to take care of," I said, indicating my phone. "Better to do it now than when we're at the cabin with the entire team, right?"

"Totally. And on that note, I'm going to send *one* more message, then I'll go offline."

I fiddled with my phone, checking out the local news, the weather forecast for the weekend, and if anyone had posted any new chapters on the writers' forum while I waited for his reply to come through.

DD: *I see you've certainly thought a lot about why you like M/M so much. Maybe I'm too much of a prude to try it. Or…could you perhaps guide me toward a good one? On the soft side, please, to start me out.*

Lily: *Aww, you'll let me help you pop your M/M cherry? That's so sweet. Give me a little time, though. This requires some thought…*

SIXTEEN

Retreat! Retreat!

THREE HOURS LATER, the men had made lasagna, we'd all devoured it, the women had done the dishes, and we were currently enjoying our drinks in front of the fireplace which Olivier had managed to light up in less than three minutes. I sat snuggled in the saggy sofa next to Sylvie, listening to her needles' hypnotic *tic, tic, tic* as she knitted. On my left Mathieu had squeezed himself into the other corner of the couch, leaving room for *almost* one person between us.

I'd be offended he sat so far away from me, but he was here before me and I was the one to choose to sit almost on top of Sylvie instead of in the middle.

Guys had this effect on me.

I couldn't remember a time where I'd been able to have a normal and relaxed conversation with a guy. They'd always seemed to be alien to me, with weird interests and loud voices and a too-straightforward way of interacting with each other. I'd never been able to anticipate their behavior and that might be one of the reasons they fascinated me so much.

I really *liked* guys. Found a large number of them highly attractive. Dreamed for hours about what it would be like to kiss them, to be held by them.

But it was out of the question to do *anything* that could possibly bring any of that about.

It was entirely possible I'd told DD too much about myself on the forum so that I'd never be able to so much as *think* about telling him the truth.

Sealing the door shut so I wouldn't have the possibility of opening it.

A couple of minutes ago, Denis vacated his chair and went upstairs where all the bedrooms were located. He was sharing a room with Mathieu. Right next door, I was sharing with Sylvie, in one of the cabin's two double beds.

The guys on the team had a collective freak-out when they discovered not all the rooms had twins. The world had come a long way in recent years, but straight guys still freaked out at the idea of sharing a bed with another straight guy.

They'd all been saved when Sylvie offered for us girls to take one of the doubles, and Tristan, of all people, offered to share the other one with Fidi.

Tristan was becoming very well-loved on the team, mostly because of the way he handled Fidi's odd ways. I was pretty sure this last action would earn him a permanent position in the hall of fame.

Fidi had been moving around all evening, spending no more than fifteen minutes with each person. I guessed he wanted to get to know everyone in a more relaxed setting than the office.

It's never easy being the new guy.

Right now, he moved to take Denis' vacated seat. He wasn't very steady on his feet, making me guess that wasn't his first beer of the evening. He sat down next to Louis, a guy who'd been on the team for only a month less than me, but who I didn't know at all.

Ten seconds later, Denis returned, with a Kindle in his hand.

"Are we that boring, Denis?" Mathieu asked. "You'd rather read a book?"

Denis' laugh was a little strained. "Figured I'd get it. Just in case." He glanced at his old seat, now occupied by Fidi.

I could understand why he'd left to get a book. On one side he had Louis, who'd had his nose in his phone since we left the dinner table—although Fidi seemed to have gotten him to turn it off for a few minutes—and on the other Kevin had his back turned to talk to Olivier.

"There's room here," Mathieu said and patted the almost-place between us on the couch. He'd noticed that Denis looked lost and didn't have anywhere to sit down. "We'll make room for you."

He tried to move even farther into the corner but there wasn't really any more room to be had on that side.

I tried scooting closer to Sylvie but she pushed me right back. "Sorry, Laure. I need the space for my elbows or the knitting is going to give me tendinitis."

My eyes lifted to check out Denis' reaction but he didn't really have one. He just smiled at Sylvie and approached the couch. "No worries. I'm sure I'll fit."

He sat down, and I held my breath to make sure no sound escaped. I could feel Sylvie's gaze on me, her needles slowing down somewhat, and I *knew* she could see me blush. Hopefully, she'd think I was just that shy.

Which I guess I was.

The entire couch sank down a couple of centimeters when Denis sat down, making me almost fall onto him. We were touching from shoulder to knee and even through our t-shirts and jeans, I could feel the heat of his body.

"Sorry," Denis said. "This really is a three-seat couch, huh?"

I drew breath to say something—I had no idea what but I had to come up with something or I'd die of embarrassment—when Mathieu answered, "We're all good, man. I promise I won't jump you."

Denis chuckled in response and I felt the vibrations all the way through my body.

Turning his head in my direction, Denis' eyes flickered over my face, no doubt noting the blush that was surely covering my entire body by now. "You all right, Laure? I can grab a chair from the kitchen if you like."

"I'm fine!" I replied in a squeak.

I could *feel* Sylvie grinning next to me but thankfully, nobody else seemed to be following our conversation, including Mathieu, who'd turned to talk to Fidi.

I cleared my throat. "So what are you reading?"

"Uh." It was Denis' turn to blush. "Just…"

Asking myself what the hell I was doing, I nipped the Kindle out of his hands and opened the cover. "Maybe I've read it," I said. "I read a lot, too."

Denis' hand moved to take back his Kindle, then stopped, then twitched.

What was I doing?

If ever I needed proof that I couldn't be trusted to behave normally under pressure, this was it. I freaked out at having Denis physically near me, and I stole his Kindle with the intent of looking at what he was reading?

When I knew perfectly well that there would be mostly romance books on this thing, and that would be difficult for a guy to live down?

Denis might be the one person on the team I felt comfortable around, but this...this was like...like...like I was an *extrovert* or something.

A page of text appeared on the screen. Denis stared down at it.

I did the same.

Now what?

At the very least, we had Sylvie's attention. I had a feeling some others were watching, too, probably because I was acting so out of character.

I should give the poor man his Kindle back.

I clicked on the Home button.

Six covers with half-naked men appeared.

My first reaction: the home page of my Kindle looked exactly the same.

Second: I couldn't let anyone else see this.

"Oh, hey!" I said and clicked on one of the covers. "I've read this one." It was a book I'd read a couple of months ago but had only recently recommended to DD. It had a *ton* of explicit and super-hot sex scenes.

I might be a girl, but I did *not* want our colleagues to know I read erotica.

Which was—finally—when I found a way out of the mess I'd created. "I can't believe you haven't read *It* by Stephen King before now. That's, like, a classic."

I kept my eyes on the screen, flipping through the pages. Jeez, it was right in the middle of one of the hottest sex scenes of the book.

"Stopped right in the middle of the action, huh?"

What was I doing? Retreat! Retreat!

"Did it get too scary for you or did you go back to give yourself a scare with that bloody clown?"

I felt Sylvie shudder on my right. "Nobody in their right mind would read that story twice. You stopped reading, right?"

Denis' eyes were locked on the page, his face a bright red. The word "dick" must have appeared at least ten times on this *one* page and there was no doubt about me having seen it.

His eyes flicked up to meet mine for a fraction of a second. I hoped he had the time to see the apology in my eyes—but also the actual question.

Did he stop here because this was too hardcore, or had he come back to read the good stuff?

I would *never* have asked such a question of my colleague. But I *would* have asked it of DD. In fact, I would assume that DD had the hottest scenes earmarked for future reference. Somehow, the two people were merging in my head, making me a lot more forward than normal with Denis.

"I, uh…" Denis cleared his throat. "Went back to figure out why that passage gave me the chills."

"You're weird," Sylvie said, but her eyes were on her knitting.

"I'd totally do that, too," I told Denis. "I like studying the masters to figure out how they can get me to feel so, uh, freaked out." Read *hot*.

Denis' eyes lifted from the page and met mine again, for more than just a moment. His cheeks were still flaming but his lips lifted in a smile and I could see the gears turning in his head.

Yeah, yeah, I read these kinds of books, too.

"If you're such a great fan of *horror*," he said. "We should compare notes sometime. I love discovering new authors."

Which he wouldn't, if we compared reading lists, since I'd already shared everything with DD, and knew we'd read pretty much the same things.

"Sure," I replied with false cheer, making Denis frown in confusion. "That sounds great." I handed him his Kindle back and faked a yawn. "But right now I have to get to bed or I'll probably die on the hike tomorrow."

Everybody who'd heard me stared at me in surprise and I glanced at my watch. It was a quarter past ten.

"I got up at, like, five this morning," I lied, pasting on the world's fakest smile. "I'm exhausted."

Without daring to send so much as a glance in Denis' direction, I fled up to my room.

SEVENTEEN

Plain Old Laure

I STOOD IN front of the bathroom mirror for an eternity, looking into my own panicked eyes.

"What were you thinking?" I asked myself. "Grabbing someone's Kindle and snooping through it?"

I shook my head. That was such a huge *faux pas*, socially speaking. When someone reads a print book, it's glaringly obvious what they're reading, so you're allowed to ask them about it. But reading on e-readers and tablets is completely different. Nobody can see what you're reading, or the list of books you have stored on it, and if someone asks you what you're reading it's easy to simply lie.

You do *not* grab someone's tablet and snoop through it.

When I heard him flush the toilet, I was still standing in the hallway like some idiot, and the sound snapped me out of my funk.

I fled to my room.

EIGHTEEN

Totally Unacceptable Behavior

THE NEXT MORNING, I woke up with my head under my pillow and one leg thrown over Sylvie's legs next to me.

"Cuddler, huh?" Sylvie said from somewhere outside of my cocoon.

"Sorry," I mumbled and pulled my leg back to my side of the bed.

Sylvie chuckled. "No worries, honey. I don't mind a cuddle myself. I think the bathroom is free. You want to go first?"

I groaned and stretched, pulling my head out from under the pillow only to squint at the sunlight streaming in behind the pulled curtains.

"Never mind." Sylvie threw her side of the cover over on my side and jumped out of bed with a satisfied purr.

Morning people. Shudder.

I lazed in bed while Sylvie took her shower, then dragged myself up once the coast was clear. While getting ready, I replayed Denis kissing my cheek the night before over and over, never tiring of it and feeling a little *zing* run through my body every single time.

Could he be *flirting* with me?

The concept was so foreign, I hardly knew what to think. This *never* happened. From someone I actually liked, I mean.

Of course, I tended to fall for the shy and reserved guys, so the chances of them taking the first step and flirting with me—if they were even interested in the first place—were slim to none.

I froze in front of the bathroom mirror, hands about to attach today's barrette in my hair, and stared at my own reflection.

I couldn't have done that on purpose, could I? To always go for the really shy guys in order to make sure nothing would ever happen?

I thought through the list of crushes from my past—and yep, they all fit the bill.

But that was just *my type*.

Or I'd been even more scared of guys than I gave myself credit for.

What a depressing way to start the day.

On that uplifting note, I stared into my reflection, lips pursed in annoyance. "You're going to flirt back today. At least *once*. This is totally unacceptable behavior. Being a little shy *will not* stop me from having a life."

I wasn't quite sure if I believed myself, but I shoved away the doubts.

I had an entire weekend with my crush ahead of me. Surely, I could manage to flirt with him *once*?

NINETEEN

Hot Sex in Erotica Novels

I WAS ONE of the last to arrive downstairs for breakfast. Clearly, this was a team of early risers—and a good part of them were nicely hung over. People sprawled out all over the place, some in the kitchen, some at the dining table, and some on the couch in front of the extinct fireplace. Sylvie had already finished eating, and was back in her spot from the night before, knitting at top speed.

I planned to grab a croissant and a cup of tea and join Sylvie on the couch, but when I passed the kitchen counter, Denis pulled out one of those fancy long-legged chairs.

"There's an open spot here, if you want," he said, his brown eyes meeting mine and a soft smile gracing his lips. "Olivier had the world's fastest breakfast and is trying to fit in a nap before we leave."

My first reaction was to refuse. Say that I was planning on sitting with Sylvie.

But with my revelation from earlier fresh in mind, I stopped to wonder why I'd automatically refuse. If Sylvie had been the one to make the offer, I would have sat down immediately, with no hesitation. I wanted to refuse because it was Denis. And not because I didn't like him, obviously, but because *I did.*

Was keeping my crushes at a distance really this much of a reflex? Did my subconscious *want* me to stay single forever?

Well, I wasn't having it.

"Thanks, Denis," I said and returned his smile. My pulse knocking up a notch, I feigned nonchalance and parked my butt in the chair. I could do this. My subconscious was going *down*.

I had no food.

I was sitting next to Denis—who had a full cup of coffee and two slices of baguette with Nutella in front of him—and was supposed to eat breakfast, but I had no breakfast.

Maybe this was why my subconscious kept me away from my crushes.

"Let me pour you a cup of coffee," Denis said and leaned over the counter to grab a mug. "Or maybe a tea?"

I totally melted at the idea that Denis had paid enough attention at work to discover I never had coffee, only tea. I wasn't against coffee as a beverage, I just couldn't stand the taste, no matter how wonderful the side effects. My friends knew about my aversion to the brew and teased me relentlessly for it—but in a friendly, fun way. DD knew because we'd once had a *long* exchange about the effects of coffee following one of my scenes, where he'd concluded I'd never had coffee because people don't get *that* cranked up by it.

But Denis hadn't been told—at least not about Laure, only about Lily—and had figured it out from observing.

Or I was reading way too much into it, and he simply offered both to be polite.

"A green tea would be great, thank you." I was proud my voice sounded normal and not lovestruck.

"Here, have some food," he said as he passed along a basket with bread, croissants and *chocolatines*. He was out of his chair to grab the tea and hot water from the water boiler and I couldn't quite decide if I was flattered he was doing all this for me or if I should be embarrassed he was doing all the work and I was just sitting there like a princess.

He was doing it all with a huge smile on his face, so I was going to assume he didn't mind. I grabbed a croissant and bit into it, closing my eyes in bliss as the crispy buttery flakes filled my mouth.

The mug of tea arrived in front of me, and Denis sat back down in his seat. Was his chair closer than it had been a minute ago? I thought it was, because his knee was almost touching mine under the kitchen counter. If I adjusted my seat, my knee would touch his.

I adjusted my seat.

Shit, my knee was touching his knee. And how pathetic was it that this simple fact made my heart speed up and a blush rise in my cheeks?

But I loved it. Terribly innocent, especially between two people who'd read *a lot* of erotica, but it lifted my spirits like nothing else.

I was touching Denis and he'd brought me breakfast and we were going hiking together and spending the rest of the weekend together.

And I'd set a task for myself in the bathroom earlier. I was going to flirt with him today, at least once. Letting my knee bump into his might not quite qualify as flirting, but it was definitely going in the right direction.

Denis hadn't moved away either, letting his knee rest against mine, even though he had plenty of space on the other side.

I was going to go all out and *start a conversation*. I was feeling crazy; what better time to move out of my comfort zone?

"So, did you get any reading done last night?"

As the words escaped my mouth, I remembered which book he'd been reading, and I froze, with my mouth still open and the last piece of the croissant halfway to my mouth.

There's starting a conversation, and then there's provoking a discussion about hot sex scenes in erotica novels while in a room full of colleagues.

Denis' grin went from ear to ear and his eyes danced with mirth. "As a matter of fact, I did. Not on the story you spied on, though."

I flinched at his use of the word "spy," but couldn't really contradict him. Riffling through someone's Kindle definitely qualified as spying.

I snapped my mouth shut and put my croissant back on the table. "Sorry about that, by the way. I don't know what got into me."

"Hey, no harm, no foul," Denis said and took a sip of his coffee. "If what you said is true and you read the same books, I don't have anything to worry about, do I?"

I narrowed my eyes at him. "Why should you worry if I didn't read the same stuff?" Yep, we were definitely going to have a conversation about romance books without ever using the word romance.

He shrugged and leaned one elbow on the counter to turn his torso toward me. Then he turned back and lowered his elbow. Could he have changed his mind so he wouldn't have to move his knee away from mine? Or was I completely delusional?

"I don't mind owning up to what genres I like to read," Denis said. "But I prefer to do it with people who actually know what they're talking about."

"Meaning they've actually read at least one book in the genre," I supplied.

"Exactly."

"So how many people have you talked about this with?"

Denis seemed to find the bottom of his now-empty coffee cup terribly fascinating, all of a sudden. "Uh…" He cleared his throat. "You mean in real life?"

Now that the crisis of being accused of spying seemed to be over, I shoved the last piece of my croissant into my mouth and followed up with a sip of my tea. It wasn't as good as the stuff I had at home, but for a store-bought tea bag, it wasn't half bad.

"Yes, in real life." I thought of the hundreds of conversations I'd had with DD on the subject. "Real life first, then online," I added.

He gave me a look that I couldn't quite decipher, then set his mug down on the counter and folded his arms as he leaned on his elbows. "That would be one." He cleared his throat again. "Now that you know."

I gaped at him. "You've never told *anyone*? How is that even possible?"

Denis' eyes were fixed on the counter and a blush was slowly making its way up his neck. "I also read quite a bit of mystery and science fiction. When people ask what I've read recently, that's what I'll talk about." His eyes darted up to meet mine for a fraction of a second. "Nobody really realizes how much I actually read, I think. So if I'm able to give you one new book every month, nobody's going to think I'm hiding something from them."

"Well, *I* would!"

His eyes met mine again, and stayed there. "Would you, though? Or would you assume that to me, reading one book a month is 'reading a lot'?"

I pulled back—torso only, so our knees were still touching—as I forced myself to consider his words.

"Shit, you're right. I'd totally judge you for your definition, but I probably wouldn't investigate any further."

"Investigate." Denis chuckled. "You sound like you read your fair share of mystery, too."

"Maybe I do," I conceded. "Not as many, though." But enough to do exactly what Denis said. I'd been using the same tactic without even realizing it.

"I have friends who know what type of books I like to read, though. I just don't tell them the particulars, because they're making enough fun of me at it is."

"Your friends make fun of you for your taste in books?" Denis looked like he wanted to find my friends and give them a piece of his mind. Which was very sweet, and also kind of aggressive—and a bit of a turn-on.

I hurried to defend my friends. "They're not mocking me for it! It's just some good-natured ribbing. Like how we make fun of Sabrina for letting everyone at work walk all over her, though in reality, we do it to encourage her to stand up for herself because she's more than good enough. And we try to get Caroline to eat less—not because she's too fat, but because we know she sees it as something awful and insurmountable.

"They make fun of me because of my tastes, but it's partly to show me they're interested. They try to get me to tell them exactly what I like, not so they can judge me, but so they can understand me better. They want to know why I'm so set on wr— on reading that stuff."

Denis shot me a glance at my almost-slip, but luckily let it go. "Then why don't you tell them anything? If you know they actually want to know?"

I chewed on my lip, with my eyes on my tea, as I considered his words. "Guess I like my anonymity. Knowing they'd accept it is enough."

Using the pad of his index finger to pick some crumbs off the counter, Denis' voice was so low I almost couldn't hear him. "Anonymity is great. But it can also be a prison. If you wait too long, it might become impossible to get out."

TWENTY

And There'd Be Shorts

We were hiking to some sort of lake. Tristan told us the name of the place before we set off and then I promptly forgot what it was. My brain wasn't made for remembering the names of places. Besides, I wasn't in charge of this hike and was fine with that. I'd follow the rest of the team and trust them not to get us lost.

I did *notice* my surroundings, though. We parked at a pass that the cars had to work quite hard to get to, through the classic winding, narrow mountain roads. Then we took off on foot on a wide path that wound slowly up a barren mountainside, with a panoramic view of the impressive Pyrenees to our left, and, toward the end, a breathtaking view of the plains leading toward Toulouse on the right. It was enough to make anyone, even a self-declared geek, a lover of nature.

The morning nap seemed to have worked wonders on Olivier's hangover. He ran up that mountain like a gigantic goat, making me wonder how the guy ever found the time to sleep, seeing the amount of sports the guy must do to be in that good shape and have that much muscle.

The rest of us trudged along at a more sedate pace, putting one foot in front of the other as we chatted amiably and admired the increasingly fabulous view of the Pyrenees.

I also admired the view of Denis' backside.

I'd known the guy for almost a year, and had a crush on him for a few months already, so you'd think I knew what he looked like. But the thing was, we'd only ever hung out at the office—where the dress code indicated that guys cannot wear shorts.

It was the first time I'd seen him in shorts. A pair of knee-length, blue surfing shorts that clung snugly to his a-lot-firmer-than-I'd-thought ass and muscular thighs.

The novelty of actually seeing his calves, hairy and masculine, gave me the impression of seeing a completely new Denis. You were supposed to be impressed by how a guy cleaned up when he put on a suit or a uniform, not when he dressed down and went all casual. But I'd always seen Denis in the same type of clothing; jeans, a button-down shirt, and a V-neck sweater on top during winter.

Surfing shorts, hiking boots, and a snug-fitting t-shirt matching the shorts, was completely novel. And sporty—making me wonder what kind of sport he practiced. He was no Olivier, but no geek ever got that kind of leg muscles from sitting in front of his computer all day.

We walked in a single file along the narrow mountain path, and I'd taken the spot behind Denis. My eyes had been glued to his butt for the last half hour and I didn't see that changing any time soon. It got even worse when the incline increased, and his ass was naturally at my eye level.

I'd had a crush on Denis when I thought he was just a regular geek, who was really good at his job and who probably spent all his free time in front of his computer at home.

Then he'd gone and cut his hair, following my advice, and making him even more handsome, exactly as I'd predicted.

Then I'd discovered he was also my online friend, DD, who I was nowhere near having a crush on, but who I felt close to, and who I'd confided in.

And now? Now I discovered he wasn't *that* much of a geek. He wasn't pasty white—at least his legs and arms were tanned—and he wasn't all skin and fat with no stamina. He was clearly an active guy…and this made him even more appealing, dammit.

Result? I was completely tongue-tied, incapable of coming up with anything to say. Around us, everyone was chatting—a comment on the view, on some plant, on someone's hangover or Olivier's impressive recovery, or on the upcoming Avengers movie—but there was no discussion between Denis and I. I talked to Sylvie behind me. He talked to Tristan in front of him.

I searched desperately for something to say but came up empty. I knew what I'd say to my friend DD—but couldn't say that to *Denis*. I knew what I'd say to my geeky colleague Denis—but couldn't bring myself to say anything to this new version of him.

So, naturally, my mouth played tricks on me again.

Fidi and Tristan stopped, Fidi turning to talk to Tristan about something, clearly exasperated. Denis turned to face me, forcing my eyes to make a *very* quick jump up from his ass to his eyes, asking, "You all right back there, Laure? Haven't heard you much."

"What kind of sport do you do?" I blurted.

Smooth.

Denis blinked. Smiled. "I play soccer."

"Oh." I gave him a once-over, arguing with myself that this proclamation surely gave me the right to—not that I could have stopped myself even if I wanted—and yes, his physique definitely fit with that sport. More legs than torso, and most likely a great runner.

"You never mentioned that," I told him. Even I can hear the confusion in my voice. Why was this guy changing in front of my very eyes all the time?

And why did I like him better with each new discovery?

Denis gave a one-shouldered shrug. "Never came up, I guess. I've talked soccer with Mathieu—he doesn't play anymore, but is a big fan of the PSG of all things—but I guess that wasn't at times when you were around?"

Frowning at whatever he saw on my face, he added, "It's not like I've hid it or anything. I just don't feel the need to tell everyone about last night's practice twice a week."

Clearly, I had lost all control of my eyes, because they took another trip down Denis' body, even though he couldn't possibly miss what I was doing. Practice twice a week. Probably plus games.

"Maybe you'd like to come watch a game sometime?" Denis asked, making my heart jump into my throat, thinking he'd read my mind.

"I mean, we're hardly pros, obviously, so it won't be like watching the Champions League or anything, and we lose more games than we win because half the team are young dads who can't take time off from the family every weekend, so we often don't even have any reserves."

God. With my inability to form words, I'd made him ramble, like he always did to fill a silence.

"You probably don't even like soccer," Denis continued, his eyes going wider by the second, either from knowing he was rambling or from embarrassment at having invited me to watch a game. "It's more of a guy thing, isn't it? Not that girls can't play or watch soccer, of course, lots do. But not that many. And I've never heard you talk about it, so you're probably not a fan. Which is why I never initiated a conversation with you about it. I—"

"I'd love to come watch a game sometime." I found my voice. Seeing how he was freaking out finally got me to get over myself. "I haven't watched a Champions League game since sometime in college when my father forced me to watch some game with him in the hopes I'd catch the soccer bug, but it might be fun if I know one of the players."

And there'd be shorts. Right?

"Great." I could see the relief flooding poor Denis now that he'd managed to stop rambling. "I'll send you the schedule. I'm one of the losers who come to every game, so you can choose whichever date works for you."

"I don't think going to all the games of your soccer team qualifies as being a loser," I told him with a smile.

Tristan and Fidi finally finished whatever had kept them busy up ahead, allowing all of us to keep moving. Olivier was so far ahead I couldn't even see him anymore.

Denis turned to follow Tristan—and my eyes went straight back to his ass.

Might as well enjoy the view.

TWENTY-ONE

Oh, You're One of Those

WHEN WE REACHED the lake that was our destination for today's hike, my head was spinning, and it wasn't due to the altitude.

Things were moving too fast for me. Things weren't supposed to be moving at all, and now I'd discovered that Denis had a lot more layers than I'd given him credit for, he'd kissed me on the cheek last night—which was *not* something a colleague or even a friend was supposed to do—and he'd invited me to come watch him play soccer.

Did that qualify as a date?

Probably not. I wouldn't even get to talk to him since he'd be on the field kicking a ball.

I'd just be watching him. In shorts.

Why was that so hard to get over? Guys wore shorts all the time. Geez.

And yet. My eyes had been on Denis' legs and ass during the entire hike. To the point where I think even Tristan, who walked in front of Denis, noticed. He hadn't said anything, thank God, only suppressed a smile and continued walking.

I felt like I was drowning in newness and in Denis, and I wasn't even close to getting a respite. There were more than twenty-four hours left of our team-building weekend.

The next two of those were to be spent at a midnight-blue lake cradled between three peaks, surrounded by painfully green grass and some dispersed boulders and a flock of ten sheep.

Tristan, Fidi, and Olivier offered some entertainment when we reached the lake, which gave me a little bit of a breather. Olivier had arrived so far ahead of us that he'd had the time to fall asleep on the grass. Tristan and Fidi somehow took this as an invitation to douse the guy in lake water. It didn't look like a very good idea while they were doing it, and Olivier's reaction when he was dunked confirmed my suspicions.

The guy proved that his muscles weren't just for show by lifting Tristan and Fidi *at the same time* and dumping them in the lake.

The result was two guys soaked and freezing and one satisfied Olivier with a small wet stain on his t-shirt. The rest of the team stood by staring, each with a plate of salad in our hands, as Tristan had asked us to empty the salad bowl in order to use it to dunk Olivier.

Guess we were eating the salad first.

With the silly stunt out of the way, my mind went back to Denis. This couldn't be healthy. He was standing down by the water, one hand holding his plate and the other helping Tristan, holding his wet clothes as he removed them.

People were settling in on the grass, spread out over a rather large area, some preferring to sit on the flat grass, others searching out stones to double as seats.

I really needed to get my head on straight around Denis. Some alone-time was in order. So I separated from the rest of the group, pretending to search for a stone that was *just* right—which was the case, but I was actually searching for a spot where nobody could comfortably sit down next to me.

I found what I was looking for no more than five meters away from Sylvie—not so far away that I'd get comments—a flat slab of rock surrounded by small, pointy ones.

I had the time to take one bite of my salad—pasta, tomatoes, eggs, and corn with some sort of homemade sauce that Sylvie had whipped up that morning—before Denis stood right in front of me.

"You don't mind sharing, do you?" he said, a warm smile on his lips. "That stone looks big enough for two, and I wouldn't want you to sit here all by yourself."

I *was* too far from the group, dammit.

Or was it an excuse on Denis' part?

I *really* needed to get out of my own head.

"I guess there's room." I scooted over to the edge of the rock and discovered that yes, there was plenty of room for two on there.

"Thanks." He sat down, letting out a satisfied sigh. "Man, I'm going to feel this in my thighs tomorrow."

My eyes took this as an invitation to stare at his legs again. Legs that were almost touching mine. Now that he was sitting, his shorts pulled up a little to show the beginnings of some quite respectable quads. The legs of a soccer player.

"Your legs look like they can take it." My blush rose at an alarming speed. Would I ever be able to reapply my filter around this guy?

Denis grinned at me. "Don't think hiking and playing soccer uses quite the same part of the muscles or something. I always feel like an old man after hiking."

Blush still flaring, I managed a smile. "Maybe you should try stretching."

A wink. "Stretching is for sissies."

"Oh, you're one of *those*." I snorted. "You don't stretch after soccer either, I imagine?"

Denis shook his head as he chewed his salad.

"You really should," I told him, and somehow, this familiar subject got my brain back online and made my blush manageable. "If I don't stretch regularly, I start feeling like a stick and everything hurts right away. Especially with an office job like ours. It's so easy to get a stiff neck or an aching back or problems with wrists or elbows. I even sleep better, since the body isn't all tense and trying to avoid the parts that already hurt and making everything even worse."

Denis was smiling at me, his eyes not leaving my face for a second while I talked. It was like we were the only people in the world, our colleagues, mere meters away, completely forgotten. I saw nothing but Denis, the impossibly blue sky, and the sun reflecting in the lake.

"You sound like you do sports only for the stretching," Denis said.

"I guess I do, in a way. I do yoga once a week with three friends. It's quite the work-out, you know, but it also has a lot of stretching. When that hour is over, I'm so mellow you could get me to agree to anything."

Denis' eyes glinted. "I'll remember that."

I laughed. "Please don't. My friends already use it against me. That's quite enough, thank you very much."

"Yeah?" Denis shifted his seat, making his hips come into contact with mine and my breath caught. "What do they get you to agree to after yoga?"

Huffing, I also adjusted my seat. I had the intention of moving away from him, to get that safe space back between us, but somehow I must have miscalculated, because now it wasn't just our hips that were touching, it was also our thighs.

My voice hitched slightly, but at least I managed to answer his question. "It's not what they get me to do, it's the answers they get out of me."

"Ah, so it's like a truth serum, too?"

"I guess you could say that. They get me to share stuff that I wouldn't normally share."

"Hmm." Denis ate another forkful of salad. "Sounds like the place to catch you, indeed. So what kind of stuff do they get you to share?"

Alarm bells were going off in my head. I could *not* allow my filter to fail me now. Telling him that they got me to talk about my crush—him—was not an option!

"Oh, you know," I hedged. "Girl stuff."

Denis chuckled and shoved another forkful of salad into his mouth. "I see."

He probably did, dammit.

"If you're serious about me needing stretching," he said with that glint in his eyes again, "you should let me come to one of your yoga sessions some time."

I, of course, had my mouth full of salad, and spit it all out. On my knees, on the grass…

"Here," Denis said with barely suppressed laughter.

And picked a grain of rice out of my hair.

TWENTY-TWO

Blanket Burrito

That night, the entire team was going out bowling. However, the cabin only had two bathrooms, so it took hours for everyone to get ready. Some, like Sylvie and Olivier, wanted to fit in a nap before we left to make sure they wouldn't fall asleep in their seats at the bowling alley. A few of the younger colleagues went off to their rooms to get their daily dose of films and social media.

I was one of those geeky types, of course, but with Sylvie napping in our room, I didn't want to bother her. I had somehow managed to be the very first person to use one of the bathrooms and once I was ready, I settled into the couch in the living room, blissfully alone.

As promised, DD's next chapter was up. It was kind of sad that I was *this* happy it was up before I had to leave for the night, but hey, I'm that kind of girl.

I settled into the couch with a blanket around me and devoured DD's chapter. Fred's discussion with his roommate had made him wonder if he was doing the right thing rushing into having sex with Laure when they still didn't know each other that well. Result: he takes her on an outing for an entire day, visiting the museum, having lunch in a romantic café, strolling along the river hand in hand… Romantic as all hell—and still no sex scene!

Damn the man.

Lily: *Where's my sex scene?*

I pressed send and almost jumped out of my skin when I heard a notification ping behind me.

With his head bent over his phone, Denis came around the back of the couch, and sat down next to me. I could bloody *see* the message going to *read* as he clicked on his phone—and a gorgeous, and slightly wicked, dammit, smile stretched across his face.

He didn't answer my message, though. He put his phone in his pocket and turned to face me. "You got an early shower, too?"

"Turns out this is a fairly gallant team. I think they let all the girls go first."

"Huh. Do you think I should take it badly that I was the first guy, then?"

I giggled and adjusted my seat so I wasn't halfway lying down on the couch, drowning in the blanket. It felt a bit too decadent with someone watching.

"I don't suppose you'd mind sharing?" Denis asked.

I looked at him blankly, not understanding *at all* what he wanted to share.

"The blanket," he said, pointing at it. "It looks big enough for two."

"Uh...sure."

What was going on? Was this normal behavior, to ask someone to share a blanket? I'd do it without hesitation with my friends. But Denis was a colleague and we were sort of at work and... And was I really hesitating about sharing a blanket with my crush? What was *wrong* with me?

With shaking hands, I pulled at the blanket, trying to get it out from under me, but failing miserably. I was *stuck* in the bloody thing and couldn't even find a corner to pull on. I tried getting up, hoping that would loosen it up a little, but I was too caught up in it to be able to stand, so I just fell back down on my ass.

"Need a hand?" Denis asked. There was definitely laughter in his voice, but it didn't feel like he was laughing *at* me.

I slumped back into my seat and threw my hands in the air. "I give up. I think you're going to have to cut me out." I managed to meet his smiling eyes. "Would you mind getting the scissors and get it over with before anyone else comes down here?"

He chuckled—and that was a sound I could *so* get used to hearing on a regular basis—and grabbed behind my back. He came back out with a corner.

"How did you do that?"

"I'm *that* talented." He was a lot closer, all of a sudden. He'd shifted across the couch to sit next to me, so close that our knees would have touched if I wasn't currently a blanket burrito.

I could smell his aftershave and something more fruity—probably his shower gel. I heard his breath going in and out, smooth and calming.

I stopped all pretense of trying to help him get me out of the blanket. I simply didn't have the mental capacity.

Denis moved his arms around me, removing the blanket bit by bit. He'd get me to move a little this way, a little that way, to free up some fold or corner. And I swear, every time I moved, we were closer together.

At least half the blanket was in his lap now, and I could probably have moved if my mind would agree to it—but yeah, no, that wasn't happening anytime soon.

I was like that bloody deer in the headlights. Except I really wanted to be run over.

He leaned close again, his arm stretched out to reach behind me, but he wasn't looking at what his hand was doing. He was looking at me, into my eyes, his gaze intent and sure.

Where was shy Denis? Who was this suave guy who'd taken his place?

And why was my mind going in *all* directions when his lips were getting closer…and closer…

He kissed me. His soft lips touched mine and I swear to God, I stopped breathing. My eyes stayed wide open.

At first I panicked. Genuinely panicked. Denis was kissing me! I had to kiss back! What if I didn't remember how? What if I was awful?

Needless to say, with all that going through my mind, I didn't even kiss him back, not really. So when our lips had been in contact for several seconds and nothing happened, Denis pulled back far enough to be able to focus on my eyes.

"I'm sorry," he said softly. "Did I misread the situation?"

He retreated a little more.

He wasn't going to kiss me again!

Finally, I remembered how my body worked. My voice, not so much, so I figured my actions could talk for me.

I threw my hands around his neck and pulled him back toward me. I pulled his mouth to mine and squeezed my eyes shut as our lips squashed together so hard I thought I might have cut my lip on my front teeth.

Denis' chuckle sounded really weird with his mouth closed. But it calmed me down enough for me to let go of my death grip and to ease up enough to actually feel something in my lips.

And once the softness of Denis' lips registered? I *finally* let go and actually kissed him.

I *did* know how to do this. My mind disconnected and my nerve endings took over, sending my hands over Denis' neck, sliding up to his stubbly head, down to his scratchy cheeks.

My lips met his, stroke for stroke, sliding along their slick surface, pulling his lower lip between mine, reveling in the softness.

Satisfied little sighs escaped my mouth but I didn't even care—because Denis was making the same ones.

While we kissed, his hands finished unwrapping me from the blanket, then went to my neck, caressing my pulse point, then sliding farther up, into my hair, catching on my barrette before grabbing a fistful of hair at the back of my head.

I loved being held like this, in his embrace, protected from the outside world.

Nothing existed but him.

Until a door slammed open upstairs and Olivier yelled for everyone to get their asses downstairs.

Like a couple of teenagers caught necking on the couch, Denis and I jumped to each side of the couch, our hands shoved between our legs and our cheeks burning. We couldn't have looked more guilty if we tried.

It was all too much, and I finally cracked and burst out laughing.

And that's how the rest of the team found me; laughing so hard I cried, folded in half on the couch, gasping for breath.

I don't deal with stress all that well.

TWENTY-THREE

We're Not Sixteen

THE DRIVE DOWN to the bowling alley was really awkward—or really hot, I couldn't quite decide. The tension was killing me, but in a good way.

I was once again at the back of Tristan's car, and so was Denis. We once again didn't exchange a word and spent the ride with our noses in our phones, like the nerdy geeks that we were.

I had to get help from the girls.

Laure: *Denis kissed me! I don't know what to do!*

Caroline: *I'd suggest kissing him back.*

Chloé: *Texting us is* not *the right option!*

Laure: *I did kiss him back! Eventually… But then we got interrupted and now we're in the car together and we're going bowling with the rest of the team and I have no idea what to say or do!*

Sabrina: *Does he know you know about his pen name?*

Caroline: *I'm getting* Friends *flashbacks. When are we doing a* Friends *marathon again?*

Chloé: *Go back to kissing him! Believe me, he's not going to complain—especially if he was the one to kiss you first.*

Laure: *I can't just jump him out of nowhere in the car. Besides, we're at work. In our boss's car. And we're not sixteen.*

Caroline: *How about a SKAM marathon? Now that the French season 4 is done, I think we owe it to the creators of that masterpiece to watch all the other remakes as well. Apparently, the German one is really good.*

Chloé: *Fine. Don't jump him. But at least don't ignore him! You can't just sit there in the car with him after having shoved your tongue down his throat and show more interest in your phone than in him. I know you're both geeks, but seriously, Laure. There should be limits to your social awkwardness.*

Laure: *You guys are no help at all. Have fun at yoga tomorrow. Try not to spend all your time talking about me.*

Caroline: *You think too much of yourself. I'm going to spend all my time talking about SKAM.*

With a sigh, I shut down my phone and shoved it into my purse. I could feel it vibrating from time to time with incoming messages, but I wasn't going to read them now. I knew how to recognize the signs of a conversation going off the rails with those girls.

I didn't actually exchange any words with Denis in the car, but we both put down our phones and from time to time our gazes met. I gave him a tentative smile and got one right back. He made a *yikes* expression and cocked an eyebrow and I couldn't help but laugh. We really had behaved like teenagers, hadn't we?

And I didn't regret it for a second.

At the bowling alley, the rest of the team had a fifteen-minute-long discussion on who should be on which team. Speculations on who knew what they were doing and who would be sore losers and who had grown up next door to a bowling alley took up everybody's attention.

Except for mine and Denis', of course.

We stood a little bit apart from the rest of the group—not so far it would seem suspect, but far enough that nobody would overhear what we were saying—and the let others decide our fates for the evening.

"You all right?" Denis asked.

"Fine," I replied. "A little…I don't even know. Weirded out?"

One side of Denis' mouth lifted. "Weirded out by kissing me? Ouch."

I snort-laughed then covered my mouth with my hand. "Sorry. That's not what I meant. You get that, right? It's just weird…that it happened, I guess?"

Denis glanced at the rest of the group, making sure we were still alone. His half-smile was still in place, thank God. "Not entirely sure you're making things better."

My heart was trying its best to hammer its way out of my chest. I was worried I'd offended him. Worried he'd change his mind and wouldn't want to kiss me again. Worried he'd kiss me again. And honestly? Kind of wondering if it had really happened.

This stuff *never* happened to me.

"I'm freaking out, all right?" I threw my hands in the air, then shoved them in the pockets of my jeans. "Not because I didn't like it, but because I wasn't expecting it, and all our colleagues are here, and there's no time to regroup."

The little lilt of the lips turned into a fully fledged smile. "The need to regroup, I can understand." Another glance at our colleagues. "How about we chill out as colleagues tonight and then discuss what happened earlier once we're alone?"

I could actually feel the tension leaving my body. "That sounds great. Maybe tomorrow after we get back to Toulouse?"

"Tomorrow night it is." With a wink, he strolled over to talk to Mathieu.

I could breathe a little easier—until I realized I'd just set up a ticking clock. Now I had almost twenty-four hours to stress and worry about what would happen once we were alone.

And this is the type of situation where having a healthy imagination is not a good thing.

TWENTY-FOUR

It's Free on Sundays!

THE REST OF the weekend went by in a haze. I know we played bowling and that my team played opposite Denis' team. I know we lost, partly because Olivier is a bloody bowling god, and partly because Fidi and Tristan were playing some sort of gay chicken that made no sense to anybody on the team, but which everybody found endlessly amusing.

Then came an hour together in the back of Tristan's car, where I busied myself with catching up on the stories I was following on the writers' forum and replying to all the comments I'd gotten on my latest chapters. I didn't know what Denis was doing, but I'd venture to guess he was doing the same thing. After all, his newest chapter had come up on Saturday night and he couldn't have had much time to catch up.

The office parking lot was eerily quiet and empty on a Sunday afternoon. Everybody said quick goodbyes—we were meeting again in this very same spot tomorrow morning, after all—and took off in their respective cars.

I was parked next to Denis, so it was perfectly logical for us to walk off in the same direction.

"Could I invite you to my place for a cup of coffee or tea or something?" Denis asked. "*Just* a cup of tea, mind. I'm not propositioning you or anything. Just wanted to offer a place to talk that's not a parking lot. But I'm not coming on to you or anything. Unless you want me to. Gah!" He covered his face with his palm.

Awkward Denis was back!

I was so relieved I giggled. Nervous reaction. "A cup of tea sounds great," I told him. "You live in the city center, right? I'll follow you. But would you mind texting me the address in case I lose you on the way?"

Apparently, awkward Denis meant confident Laure. And confident Denis meant nervous and awkward Laure. Would we ever manage to get the both of us confident at the same time?

Or would we end up on two times awkward?

Guess we wouldn't know until we tried.

I followed his blue Peugeot 207 into the city center and miraculously found a parking space right in front of his building. It was a paying space, but that was pretty much inevitable these days.

The question, of course, was how long I should pay for. My head was doing Masters-level calculations including probabilities and contingencies when Denis yelled, "It's free on Sundays!" from down the street.

Well, that solved that problem.

Denis lived in the Chalets neighborhood, which was one of the more expensive ones in the city, but the building was quite old so it didn't have an elevator. I followed him up three flights of stairs, letting my hand slide along the worn wood of the banister, placing my feet in the indents made in the stone steps by thousands of feet before me, and trying to get a grip on the excitement and nervousness building in my chest.

"This is me." Denis unlocked his door and went in first, turning on the light.

I followed his lead and removed my shoes in the hallway before padding after him into a small but cozy living room. One wall had red bricks—which is really a solid classic in Toulouse and really pretty—and two windows showed the tops of what I thought might be a plane tree in the building's backyard.

Denis went straight over to open both windows, letting in the mild spring air, accompanied by birdsong and the distant murmur of cars.

He had a shabby two-seat couch with a battered coffee table facing a shiny new flatscreen TV on the wall. A small kitchenette with a small stove and one of those under-the-bench refrigerators occupied the other side of the room, with a fold-out table that could accommodate four people, but would make the room really crowded.

It was tiny and cozy and clearly lived in.

"It's kind of small," Denis said, looking around his living room. "But it's just me, so…"

"I love it," I said immediately. "I wish my place was this cozy. Have you lived here long?"

"Five years." He looked at the walls, the ceiling, the kitchen, like people tend to do when talking about their own home when they're in it, seeing all the flaws and particularities that only they know of since it's *theirs*. "I bought it as soon as my trial period was over at work. Always wanted to get a place of my own."

One of his characters said that once, in a story he'd published way before I got to know him. Once we became online friends, I went through and read everything DD had ever published.

Buying a flat in the center of Toulouse was pretty expensive. Considering the neighborhood, I was impressed he'd managed a place with a separate bedroom—at least that's what I assumed the door next to the kitchenette led to, because the living room had nothing resembling a bed.

Don't think about beds.

"So…tea?" Denis had his hands in his pockets, nervous energy radiating off him in waves. In a way, I was relieved to see I wasn't the only one, but how were we to get anywhere if neither of us was in confidence mode?

"Herbal, if you have it," I replied and decided to sit down on the couch. The material was worn in both seats and on the armrest closest to the door, but it was comfortable. While Denis prepared two cups of herbal tea, I fiddled with my barrette and looked out the window, hoping the gentle swaying of the plane tree would bring me the calm I needed.

It didn't, of course, but it kept me occupied.

"So," Denis said as he put a steaming cup on the coffee table in front of me. "Um." He sat down on the couch with me—it's not like there were many other options, unless he wanted to sit in the kitchen at the other end of the room—and cradled his own cup.

I couldn't help but grin at him. "'Um' pretty much sums it up, yeah."

He let out a laugh. "God, this is awkward. I'm so sorry."

"Hey, it's not your fault we were interrupted." To hide my rising blush, I grabbed my mug—it was a Star Wars mug, proving

I was in the house of a true geek—and took a sip of the tea. Red berries of some sort. Nice.

Denis cleared his throat. Took a sip of his tea. Cleared his throat again. "The choice of moment to start things *was* my fault, though."

I tipped my head from side to side, considering. "I guess so. But you can't plan for these things to happen. That takes all the fun out of it." This was a regular topic of mine, but only when talking to writing friends—or to friends who read a lot, if I was in a pinch—and Denis wasn't officially a writing friend. So I forced myself to shut up.

"For example," Denis said, his voice low and soothing, "right now would be a much better time."

My eyes flew to his. There was that deer-in-headlights feeling again. But, you know, in a good way.

"Or would now *not* be a good time?" He held my gaze, the sincerity of his question clear.

"I think yesterday was pretty good timing," flew out of my mouth.

Uh-oh, filter was off.

"I mean, if that hadn't happened yesterday, we wouldn't be here now, so this situation would never have occurred. It's two different branches; one where it happened once and has the potential to happen again, and one where it never happens at all."

Denis' gaze kept boring into me with an intensity I'd never seen in the guy before. Then again, I'd probably never kept eye contact for this long before, having a tendency to look away whenever things got too intimate.

"I'm not a fan of your theory that it would never have happened, ever, if it hadn't happened yesterday—new chances can be created, you know—but we can get to that later. Right now—" his eyes glinted with hot promise "—I'd like to focus on the potential of things happening again in the reality we're in right now."

Confident Denis was definitely back.

Not allowing myself to back down, I winked—actually *winked*! "That all depends on what happens next, doesn't it?"

Who was this girl and how could I become like her more often?

Denis, bless the man, took the challenge. Never breaking eye contact, he put his mug on the coffee table, then reached out to do the same with mine. When he grabbed it, his fingers slid over mine.

It was such a cheesy and cliché move. But now that it was happening *to me*, and I could feel his skin against mine and the intent behind the touch, I totally understood the appeal.

Exactly like in his writing, Denis pulled off the cliché.

My mug landed on the table with a thunk and when Denis' hand came back, he placed it on my armrest, effectively blocking my escape.

As if I'd want to escape.

"I think this is pretty much where we were at when we were so rudely interrupted," he whispered.

I could smell his aftershave and even caught a whiff of the same fruity scent as the night before. "I don't think you were quite that far away."

Denis grinned. And leaned in and kissed me.

TWENTY-FIVE

Confused and Happy

WE PICKED UP right where we left off the night before.

His lips on mine, my hands on his neck, his hands in my hair. I didn't even register where the rest of his body was until his knee hit my hip and his other leg bumped into my knee. He couldn't have been in a particularly comfortable position, but I couldn't bring myself to care.

I was kissing Denis again, and this time there would be no interruption. I pulled at his lower lip and felt the tip of his tongue. I opened up, and a full-on battle started between our tongues.

A frustrated growl escaped Denis and his lips moved away from mine. "This is killing my neck," he said breathlessly. He grabbed my hand in his and gave a gentle pull. "Would you mind coming over here instead?"

All shyness had been kissed out of me, so I came eagerly. As he sat back in the couch, I straddled his lap and sat down on his knees.

He lost no time in shoving his hands back into my hair and pulling me to him. I winced as our lips met, because he'd accidentally pulled my hair by bumping into the barrette.

"Mind if I remove this?" he asked.

I shook my head. I wanted to keep kissing him, but it was in everybody's best interest to let him see what he was doing, so I stayed still and watched his eyes as he worked.

"A lily again," he commented with a smile. The barrette came off with a soft *click* and Denis leaned forward, bringing me with him, to place it carefully on the table.

Finally, the kissing could resume.

I lost all track of time and space; the only thing that mattered was that I had Denis under me, with me, kissing me, and that was exactly as I wanted it.

His hands traveled from my hair, to my waist, to my hips, and back to my neck. His lips kissed and nipped and licked, accompanied by soft groans and breathless sighs. Some of those noises might have been mine, I couldn't tell anymore.

My hands did some exploring, too, but it all stayed very PG-13. I had no compunction about exploring his chest, for example, but the shirt stayed on. And I felt no need to go below the belt. Not tonight.

DD/Denis couldn't have been more wrong in his assumption that my sex life was like that of my characters. Where they jumped into bed as soon as possible, I needed more time.

Like Denis.

I actually stopped and sat up straight at the realization that I *knew* that Denis wouldn't want this to go much further, either.

He'd told me as much. *I've decided not to sleep with anyone else unless I have real feelings for them.*

Now, I didn't think it would be presumptuous to assume he *did* have feelings for me. But what he said meant that he wouldn't want to have sex on a first date.

"What?…" Denis looked up at me like he was coming out of a dream, confused and happy. "Is there something wrong?"

"Nope!" I grinned. Leaned down to smack another kiss on his lips. "But I should get going, or getting up tomorrow will be torture."

Denis turned his head to read the time on the microwave in the kitchen. Half past ten. "You're right." He shook his head as if trying to get rational thought to work again and my heart soared at the knowledge that I was the one to have derailed him in the first place.

With anybody else, this would have been such an awkward moment to go through. I'd assume that the guy would want things to go further, but wouldn't be willing to, so I'd be all apologetic about it, but still would take off.

Now, with the knowledge that Denis was also someone who liked to take it slow, I was able to get out of his lap with a huge smile on my face, pick up our half-empty mugs of cold tea and bring them to the kitchen, and look him in the eye as I said my goodbyes.

Chloé had been totally right about using the inside information I had on Denis to my advantage.

"This was nice," I said. "We should do it again sometime." I must have had the largest shit-eating grin on my face *ever*.

"We should." He stood leaning against the wall in his hallway, hands in his pockets—but in a relaxed way and not nervously like earlier—a smile playing on his lips. "How about a movie Wednesday night?" Before I could answer, he added, "I'd suggest tomorrow, but I have football practice and on Tuesday I have to help a friend who's moving."

We sealed the deal with a kiss and I skipped down the three flights of stairs, my heart light and my lips replaying what had just happened over and over.

Only when I reached my car did I realize we hadn't discussed how we should handle this at work.

TWENTY-SIX

Come Back!

Laure: *I spent an hour making out with Denis on his couch!*

Caroline: *Congrats! That's so cool!*

Chloé: *Only making out? Why did you stop there? Please tell me you're still there and just taking a break to keep us updated on your progress.*

Sabrina: *Have you told him you know yet?*

Caroline: *Don't pressure her to have sex, Chloé. We can't all be like you.*

Laure: *Thank you, Caro. I will not have sex on the first date.*

Chloé: Technically, yesterday was the first one. First kiss, anyway. So why didn't you?

Laure: Because it was perfect the way it was.

Caroline: Aww!

Sabrina: Did you tell him, Laure? You can't let it get any further before you tell him. You're breaking his trust.

Chloé: Stop being a bore, Sab! Let her do her necking and kiss-and-tell in peace.

Laure: Maybe I don't need to tell him I know.

Sabrina: That's as good as declaring the relationship dead before it even starts. You've never told us what your author name is, and that's fine since we're just your friends. But even we know that you write. And a boyfriend is someone you would also tell that to. Would you never tell him about it? He's going to find it highly suspicious if you never give any details—especially since he actually reads and writes romance, too. What if he shows you his stories? What do you do then?

Chloé: You're such a buzz-kill, Sab. See, now you've scared her away. Laure! Come back!

Laure: I'm here.

Sabrina: You have to tell him, Laure.

Laure: I know. I just need to find the right time.

TWENTY-SEVEN

Where Would That Leave Me?

Monday morning had me arriving at work way more stressed out than usual. I didn't know how Denis wanted to play this out with our colleagues and I needed to figure out what *a good time* would be to tell Denis I knew he was DD and I was Lily.

I *knew* Sabrina was right. God knew I'd read enough books where the hero tried to withhold information—which never worked out in the hero's favor. If I wanted this thing with Denis to work out, wanted to take it seriously, I'd need to come clean.

But how?

I'd always shied away from confrontation, but this was even worse than telling the neighbor he'd been parking in my spot for the past two months and would he please park his car elsewhere. This was telling him I was a writer, telling him I wrote romance, telling him he'd already read all my stories and I'd read all of his. Telling him I had a crush on him.

And even if he'd also admitted, indirectly at least, to having a crush on me, that didn't make it any easier. This was putting myself out there in a way I'd never done before.

Maybe it was too soon? Sabrina was right that if this relationship was to have any kind of long-term future, I'd need to come clean. But what if it didn't work out? What if, a week from now, we broke up? Where would that leave me?

With a guy who knew way too much about me, that's where. One who worked in the same office as me, no less.

I should make sure the relationship would be worth it first. Make sure Denis was someone I could trust with my secrets, and someone I'd want to spend more time with.

Then I could accidentally discover that our online aliases knew each other.

That problem solved, I approached my office door with a little less trepidation.

It was still early, so I *should* have been the first one there. I gently pushed the door open, holding my breath like I was in a horror movie, and peeked around the room.

Denis was already there, pulling his laptop out of his backpack. Nobody else was there yet.

"Morning," I said, way too cheerfully for a Monday morning, pushing the door closed behind me. We hardly ever closed the door when somebody was there, but I suddenly realized we might have a few minutes together alone before the rest of the guys arrived, which would allow us to agree on how to behave with the rest of the team.

He looked up at me with a huge smile and my heart made a *thump* in my chest. "*Bonjour, ma belle.*" He got up and rushed right up to me, planting a huge kiss on my mouth.

"Uh," I said when he pulled back, his hands holding my face like it was something precious.

He glanced at the closed door behind me and down at my hands hanging limply by my side. The smile dimmed a little, turned bittersweet. "We're not ready to tell the rest of the team yet?"

"Uh." As his hands fell away from my face, at least I was able to think again, and attempt forming a sentence. "Please don't be offended, all right? It's not that I'm embarrassed by you or anything." Quite the contrary, in fact. "But I'm really shy and hate having people's attention, even if it's positive. I just…I guess I'd like for us to get to know each other and figure things out before our colleagues start butting in."

I took a deep breath, closing my eyes. I really *hated* confrontations.

"Hey." Denis pulled my chin up with a finger, inciting me to open my eyes to look at him. "I don't mind. I'm not exactly an extrovert myself. We'll keep it a secret for now, all right? And we'll hang out after work Wednesday. If you're still on for a movie?"

"Of course I'm still on for a movie." I smiled and even worked up the courage to go up on my tippy-toes to kiss him. "Thank you."

"My pleasure." As we heard steps arriving in the hallway, we stepped apart, Denis going to his chair to open his laptop and me pulling out of my jacket. "In any case, I love secrets," Denis said with a wink just as the door handle went down.

Yeah. Me, too, *normally*. But Sabrina's comments came rushing to the forefront of my brain, reminding me that not all secrets were fun ones.

TWENTY-EIGHT

You'd Think I Was a Girl or Something

Working next to Denis for the next two days, with our secret between us, was both fun and nerve-racking. I wasn't worried the team would find out, but I kept wondering what would happen at the movies on Wednesday night. What would it be like to go out with Denis? Was he the type of guy who would want to hold hands in public, or the type who found that stupid? Would he buy my movie ticket or would I get to pay for myself? Would we actually be watching the movie or was it all an excuse to make out for two hours?

I realized that even with the insider's information from DD on the writers' forum, I didn't know Denis all that well.

Wednesday night arrived and I spent fifteen minutes in front of my bathroom mirror trying to figure out which barrette would fit the best with the red summer dress I'd chosen. Then I decided I really wanted the white lily, but wasn't sure it went with the dress, so I changed the dress.

You'd think I was a *girl* or something. I *never* behaved like this.

Usually I posted a new chapter on Tuesdays, but with the outing that weekend and endless hours spent daydreaming about Denis, I'd missed a post for the first time in over a year.

When my readers asked if anything was wrong, I finally managed to wrap my head around writing again, and I got the chapter ready by Wednesday. Even though it meant I might be running late, I made my post—apologizing for the delay and thanking everyone for checking in on me—before running out the door. As I rushed to the metro, I felt my phone buzz with notifications from my usual readers, quick to catch up as always.

I wondered if Denis had seen it.

Probably not, since he should be on his way to the movies, like I was.

When I arrived at our meeting place—the fountain in the middle of Place Wilson, right next to the merry-go-round—Denis still wasn't there, so I checked the notifications.

My eyes went straight to the one from DD.

He'd taken the time to read my chapter *and* comment on it and was therefore—I checked the time on my phone—four minutes late?

I was both offended and flattered. This double identity stuff was messing with my head.

I clicked on the comment.

> **DD**: *Loved the chapter! Will comment more later, but right now I have to run. Am already five minutes late for the movies!* Bises.

Heat rose in my cheeks at the idea of kisses from Denis—clearly, it was going to take me a while to get used to that one. Smiling, I typed in a reply.

Lily: *Enjoy! Let the girl pay for her own ticket, by the way. Gallantry is all very nice, but sometimes it just makes you feel guilty.*

I heard the *ping* of an incoming message at exactly the moment when Denis said, "Sorry I'm late," rushing up to me from behind the merry-go-round. He must not have come by metro.

Huge smile in place, he placed a hand on the small of my back and pulled me in for a kiss.

Kissing in public was *totally* something I liked. Which I guess was a little weird, for such a shy girl, but sometimes pride in having landed the great guy takes precedence over silly hangups.

"Do you know what movie you want to see?" he asked as he grabbed my hand.

He liked holding hands in public. Grin.

I squeezed his hand, enjoying the fact that it was so much bigger than mine and had some calluses. A guy's hand. "I don't even know what movies are on these days," I said truthfully. "Anything will do. Except horror. I don't do horror." Even the idea of hiding against Denis' chest couldn't get me to willingly watch a horror movie.

"Horror isn't really my thing, either," Denis said, pulling his phone out of his pocket to check his—my—message.

Which reminded me…I already knew he didn't like horror. We'd talked about it on the writers' forum. We'd both been branded by the same film—*The Blair Witch Project*—and swore never to put ourselves through that again.

We strolled away from the fountain with its statue writer sitting seriously in the middle, past the horses of the merry-go-round running in circles with kids on their backs, across the street of the roundabout circling around the entire Place Wilson, and stopped on the pavement in front of the cinema to study the posters.

Denis pointed to one on the left. "Romantic comedy?"

Again, the double personality gave me trouble. Lily wanted to laugh with DD and say that was exactly their kind of movie and this was why we were such good friends. Laure wanted to make fun of her male colleague for proposing a chick flick.

I was simply brimming with prejudice, wasn't I?

"That looks great."

At the ticket booth, Denis turned to me. "I'd love to pay your ticket, but if you prefer to go Dutch…?"

I shouldn't have been this surprised that he took into account what I told him in my message on the forum. I *saw* him read it. And yet, my heart warmed up my entire chest because he asked the question.

"Or…" Denis glanced into the back of the hall behind the ticket booth. "I get the tickets and you get the snacks."

I couldn't have stopped my smile from stretching across my face even if I'd wanted to. "Deal."

I asked him what he wanted and made my way to the small stand selling snacks and drinks. While I waited my turn, my phone vibrated with a notification.

DD: *Thanks for the tip! Seems to be working.*

There were still two guys ahead of me in line; I had the time to type out a quick reply.

Lily: *Excellent! Now, feel free to completely ignore the film and spend your time necking during the movie!*

When I met up with Denis at the bottom of the escalator leading up to the theaters, I had my hands full with two sodas and one medium-sized popcorn. Denis put his phone in the front pocket of his jeans and relieved me of the Fanta and the popcorn. That's the type of gallantry I can get behind.

"So you figured it out, huh?" he said, his gaze oddly piercing.

I froze, the realization that something was happening that I didn't understand making my heart speed up and old self-defense mechanisms from high school slam into place. "Figure out what?"

He studied my eyes for a moment, his gaze going from one to the other like he was watching a tennis match. A slight smile made an appearance. "Lily always assumed that DD was a girl. Always talked about boyfriends and good-looking guys and what she saw in various male characters. Yet now she's giving advice on how to go on a date with a girl."

The world stopped spinning for a second. My heart stopped, my breath caught. Blaring alarms were going off in my head, saying *Abort! Abort!*

Denis knew I was Lily.

TWENTY-NINE

Why Didn't You?

"You know?" I knew it was a stupid question, but those were the only words that formed in my head right then.

Denis nodded. He was still looking at me very closely, as if he was expecting me to flee at any moment.

He had a valid point.

"How long?" I clutched my soda in both hands because my fingers were feeling numb and I didn't want to drop it and splatter us both. I had enough emotions to handle right now as it was.

The wince wasn't pronounced, but I saw it. "Uh. For a while?"

My eyes narrowed. "How long is 'a while'?"

He took a deep breath. "Since the end of your first week with the team?"

I couldn't feel my feet. Or my hands. I knew they were cold, because of the soda, but it didn't register.

He'd known. Basically, since the very first time we met, he'd known about my online alter ego. During all those goofy talks we'd had in the office, he'd known about Lily and her stories—and her insecurities, hopes, and dreams.

I'd told DD *everything* on that forum. That's the beauty of online friends, after all. You can tell them anything and not worry about the consequences. You don't have to worry about looking them in the eye the next day because you never meet face to face. If they don't react in a good way, you can just block them and pretend they never existed.

I'd told DD about my fears about starting in my very first job. I'd told him what I thought of all our colleagues—Olivier having too much muscle for my tastes, Sylvie being super nice and smart but therefore frankly intimidating, Denis being so nice and sweet and smart and sexy—expecting that information to stay top secret and online.

He'd *read all my stories.*

I loved reading and writing romance. I loved the tension, the buildup, the awkward moments, and the happily ever after. I loved the sex scenes.

And now my male colleague who I'd kissed and who I was on a date with for the first time *knew* all this.

I hadn't even told my closest friends about my pen name. I didn't feel secure enough for them to know everything. And they were *my friends*. Whom I trusted more than anyone.

"Laure?" Denis' voice seemed distant, like I was under water, drowning in shame and embarrassment. "You all right?"

I wheezed in reply. It was supposed to be a yes, but even I wouldn't have believed that.

"I realize I should have told you earlier," Denis said. I thought he was trying to catch my gaze, but my eyes refused to focus on anything and zoned out completely while aimed toward the floor.

"I, uh...I saw you were logged onto the writers' forum one of your first days and took note of your user name. I was just too curious. And incredulous that I'd actually met someone who hung out on the same forum."

That, I could believe. It's like breaking the fourth wall in cinema, except in real life.

"So I found your account and started reading your stories. I figured that if they were all crap, I'd laugh at it by myself and never mention it to anyone. Possibly block you, so you wouldn't be able to find me."

My hands spasmed at the very idea of him laughing at my stories.

"But they weren't crap. They were really good. So I found myself reading everything you'd put out over the course of one weekend, leaving comments on all the chapters I liked best."

I remembered that. New comments would pop up from time to time on an old story, as someone went through the backlist. Usually, I'd respond and move on. But DD had clearly gone through *everything*, leaving wonderful compliments and a couple of constructive criticisms. My curiosity had been piqued enough that I went over to her—his, her, I was getting confused again—homepage and started reading her stories.

Denis seemed to be on his way into rambling mode again, but I was unable to do anything about it this time. I was *way* beyond rambling, probably closer to catatonic.

"I was so happy when I saw you reading my stuff, too. I've never had anyone I know read my stories, obviously, and, I don't know. I guess it made the feedback feel more real, somehow. I knew you weren't giving fake likes so I'd like you back, or being polite. You became a friend."

My head nodded, without checking in with me first. We *had* become friends. I'd been so thrilled to have met DD. Someone who wrote really well, liked the same types of stories that I did, and was really good at listening when I had to rant about something—be it in the online writing world or the real life engineering world.

Denis stopped talking, apparently taking my nod for the beginnings of a reply.

But I had nothing to say.

I couldn't figure out the tail end of any of the thoughts speeding through my brain right now and didn't trust my mouth to manage anything intelligible.

I *had* to get the answer to one question, though. Gripping my soda so hard that the lid popped off and fell to the floor and a few drops fell on my hand, I forced out my question. "Why didn't you say anything?"

A pause, where we just stood there, looking at each other while people milled around us, taking the escalator upstairs as our movie was announced to start in five minutes. Denis stood stock still, his breath seeming to come in short bursts.

"Why didn't you?" he whispered.

My hand spasmed and I sent half my soda to the floor, splashing it on both our feet.

I fled.

THIRTY

I'd Trusted the Anonymity

Why didn't I tell Denis that I knew he was DD?

To protect myself, of course. Why does any shy person ever do anything? Before any action is validated by that part of our brain, it's gone through meticulously in search of possible weak spots or areas that are vulnerable to attack, and if the calculated risk is too high, the action receives a no-go.

I sat in the metro, all alone in the group of seats in the back, with a view of the black tracks disappearing into the dark behind us, the evenly spaced lights on the vaulted walls largely insufficient to light up the tunnel. I still held the soda cup, now empty, keeping it in a death grip as if letting it go would make me fall into a million little pieces.

Maybe it would.

I'd never felt so exposed. Not when my "friends" left me standing all alone in the middle of the school yard in eighth grade, only to yell all the secrets I'd told them so the whole school would hear. Not when the gym teacher made me stand in front of the class at the swimming pool and demonstrate how to do a proper breast stroke just because I had been a swimmer since I was five.

Both those situations had been awful, and made me even more wary of giving away any kind of information to people around me, even the ones I trusted.

I'd trusted DD. And I'd trusted in the anonymity of the internet.

Now there was a guy, who I had to work with every day, and who was quite possibly pissed at me right now because I'd run out on him without a word, who knew way too much.

I *couldn't* own up to loving romance at work. I just couldn't.

Nobody would understand. In France, it was bad enough if you didn't read the literary snobbery we studied in school. Reading mystery, for example, was *barely* acceptable as a pastime, but not really qualified as *reading*. It was basically the equivalent of watching reality TV. Not something to brag about.

But romance? And from a girl who'd been single since the first day she set foot in that office? Who's not particularly pretty or witty?

Loser.

Pathetic.

I curled in on myself, leaning down so my head was between my knees. I wanted to disappear. Go back in time and never take the job. Never open the forum in the workspace. Never interact with DD.

I finally managed to let go of the paper cup so I could put both hands over my face. The cup clattered to the floor.

"There's a trash can right there," an angry male voice said.

"Sorry," I mumbled. I uncurled, grabbed the cup, and stood up to throw the cup in the trash. The metro pulled into a station—not quite mine yet, but who cares—and I got off.

Nothing like the threat of a confrontation to get me moving.

THIRTY-ONE

Never Again

I SHOULD NEVER have accepted to go to the movies on a Wednesday. Movies are for weekends. So you have a day or two to recover after.

I had no such luxury and had to show up at work on Thursday morning, no matter that I hadn't slept a wink and spent the entire night poring—yet again—over all the messages I'd exchanged with Denis on the writers' forum over the past months.

I'd given away *so much*.

Never again.

When the idea hit at eight this morning, I realized I was too tired to do anything about it, but the knowledge that there *was* something I could do helped me find the courage to get into the shower and take off for work.

Nothing forced me to stay in this job, after all. I could go somewhere else. Toulouse was a big city and had thousands of jobs for engineers both in aeronautics and space exploration. I just needed to update my resume and put it up on a website or two, and I'd be out of there in no time.

Of course, as I pulled into the office parking lot, I realized I'd forgotten one small detail: there was a three-month notice on my contract. I couldn't just slap a letter on my boss's desk and hightail it out of there. And although it made the weight on my chest a little easier to know that the end was in sight, those three months could become pure torture. As eleven-year-old me could testify.

As I sat there, working up the nerve to get out of my car, someone pulled up next to me. It was Tristan and Fidi. They were so deep into conversation that they didn't even see me sitting there before practically running toward the main entrance.

A new idea started to form. Those two had been with the company for years, but had only recently transferred to my project. The fact that I needed this reminder only proved how out of sorts my brain was, but suddenly, a new door opened for me.

I could ask to change projects. That could take a lot less than three months. After all, Tristan and Fidi had been parachuted here from their old projects in a day or two. Why not do the same for me?

Taking a deep breath, I forced myself to open the door and step out.

And go to work.

THIRTY-TWO

You Guys Are Cute as Hell

"You want to change projects." Tristan looked at me from across the meeting room table, his gaze flat and his hands folded in his lap.

"Yes."

"Today. You want to move to a different project. Today?"

"Yes." I wondered if there was something wrong with Tristan for him to have such a neutral reaction. It's not like it was that uncommon for someone to ask to change projects from time to time. It was even encouraged by management.

Tristan was obviously waiting for something from me, but I had no idea what. "I just thought it might be time to try something new. I'd really like to try my hand at mobile apps—"

"You've worked for us for less than a year, Laure. People usually stay for at least a year or two before moving on to something else." He sighed. "I find it a little…suspicious…that you're asking this *today*."

Okay, I was definitely missing something. "What's so special about today?" I ask tentatively.

He sighed again and ran a hand through his hair. "Did you not follow what was going on here yesterday at all?"

Yesterday? Oh!

I'd been so absorbed in my own life and looking forward to going to the movies with Denis, I'd hardly registered the impromptu team meeting in the afternoon. I flashed back to Tristan and Fidi arriving together this morning.

"It's not because you're gay!" I blurted out.

Smooth.

But geez. The guy had come out to us and to our homophobic client *yesterday* and here I was today announcing that I wanted to leave his team.

"That's not the reason *at all*," I almost yelled, gripping the table with both hands, panic rising. "It's a total coincidence. I think you guys are cute as hell."

I winced as I said it and my stomach dropped as I saw the expression on Tristan's face. I wasn't sure if it was embarrassment or anger, but neither was good.

"God, I'm sorry, I didn't mean it like that. But really, that's not why I want to change. Really."

Tristan folded his arms over his chest as he stared me down. "All right. What is the reason, then? Because I'm not buying the kid fresh out of school having already learned all there is to learn on a project like this and wanting new challenges. Last I saw, you still call on Denis at least twice a week. Which is a good thing, by the way," he added belatedly.

I could feel my blush rising at the mention of Denis. I didn't have an answer for him. He was right about me not having learned all there was to learn on the project, and I couldn't even tell him I had a much more interesting project in view, since I hadn't gotten that far yet. I'd somehow assumed that *Tristan* would be the one to find one for me.

I really was a rookie.

When I didn't come up with anything to say, Tristan spoke again. "Fidi is pretty confident that he caught our data thief."

Right. Tristan told us on Monday that someone had gotten their hands on the database our tool worked on and they were working on finding the culprit. The information hadn't made much of a bleep on my radar. First, because I was too caught up in daydreaming about Denis. And second, because I didn't see what that had to do with me. I just corrected bugs. I hardly ever touched that database and barely understood what the different elements were.

"But the police will have to do their job, and in the meantime, we're staying extra vigilant."

I nodded my agreement, although I failed to understand the change of subject.

"I'm *really* curious, Laure, as to why you want to jump ship *today*." Tristan's gaze locked onto mine, his lips in a severe line. Tristan was only my second boss, but he'd given me a very good first impression. Professional and competent, but also funny and nice. The guy sitting opposite me right now didn't look very nice. And he was definitely not laughing.

Finally, my brain caught up. "You think *I* stole the database?" I felt my mouth hanging open and snapped in shut.

"I don't know," Tristan said. "Did you?"

"No! Of course not!"

"Then why do you want to leave?"

I briefly thought about telling him the truth—the guy was in a relationship with a colleague, he might even understand—but there was no way. It was bad enough that Denis knew too much about me. I couldn't add Tristan to the list. Even with my job on the line, I kept quiet.

There were other jobs. I only had the one heart.

As the silence lengthened, Tristan's forehead folded into a frown. "I have no idea what's going on here, Laure. Should I still pass on to Dimitri that you want to change teams?"

Dimitri. Tristan's boss and quite frankly intimidating with his suits and wire-rimmed glasses and cool demeanor. Who would ask me the same questions. Which I would still not have any answers to.

I shook my head.

"So you're staying?" He leaned forward, placing his elbows on the table. "I don't want to pressure you to stay if you're unhappy with us, Laure. I hope that if you have problems with anybody on the team, you know you can come to me, right? If somebody's not treating you right, it's not you who should change teams, but them."

I cleared my throat to get my voice to work. "Nobody's bothering me. This is the best team ever."

"And yet you want to leave."

I dropped my eyes to the table, unable to find an answer that my mouth would accept to let through its filter.

After a minute or two, Tristan got up and left.

THIRTY-THREE

You're Right There

When I got back to my desk, Denis had arrived.

He turned on his chair to face me when I came through the door, but I kept my eyes on my own chair and walked right past him, sat down, and popped on my headset. Quick, I linked it to my phone and started a Spotify playlist.

I couldn't face him right now. Couldn't talk to him.

I had no way of controlling what came out of his mouth, but I *could* attempt to get him to not talk to me at all.

So I focused on my tasks for the day—yet more bugs, one that was just a question of changing a text color and one more complicated—and only on that. I'd never been so efficient my entire life.

I never took my eyes off my screen, but at one point I did notice that Denis left his seat, probably for a coffee break. When he came back, he tried to talk to me but I pretended not to hear him because of the music. He stared at me for a while, but eventually went back to working.

At a quarter to twelve the usual group chat popped up, asking who was getting their lunch at the food truck outside.

Most days, almost everyone from the team—except for one guy who lived five minutes on foot from the office and one girl who went jogging every single lunch break—ate together in the lunch room. Some brought food from home, but the majority was too lazy and ordered from the food truck or one of the numerous *boulangeries* in the vicinity.

Both Denis and I usually chose the food truck. We frequently chatted while waiting our turn, sometimes about work but often about everyday stuff. It used to be one of my favorite moments of the day.

His reply was one of the first in the group chat. He was going to the food truck.

I just couldn't.

Laure: *Sorry, have an appointment. Will eat outside today.*

I could *feel* Denis turning toward me.

I continued working on correcting my bug. I kept the volume on my music loud.

And I ate a sandwich in my car, all alone, freaking out about everything and finding answers to nothing.

When I got back to the office, Denis was waiting for me. He sat in my chair, with my headset in his hands. I honestly started turning around to run back out when he started talking.

"I'd like to see you in the meeting room down the hall, Laure. If that's okay with you?"

It was *not* okay with me, of course. But when he talked, both Fidi and Tristan looked up from their computers and it was more than general curiosity that I saw in their eyes. Denis wanted to see me for a work-related reason and I couldn't reasonably refuse.

I realized that I was spiraling out of control, but I wasn't so far down the drain that I was ready to throw away my job and my career. So I forced a smile and prayed my voice wouldn't fail me. "Sure. No problem."

I dumped my things on my desk and followed Denis into the tiny four-person meeting room down the hall. He closed the door behind him.

My heart rate tripled.

"Tristan tells me you want to leave the team," Denis said, leaning against the door. His expression was closed off, professional. Emotionless.

I opened my mouth but nothing came out.

I hadn't even thought about the fact that Tristan might mention to Denis, his Tech Lead, that I wanted to leave. This was why I should learn to not listen to my panic attacks.

"He thinks you might have had something to do with the stolen database," Denis continued. "Because of the timing." He took a deep breath, let it out slowly. "I told him I really didn't think that was it. But I couldn't tell him the real reason. Or, well. Didn't think you'd want me to tell him the real reason. So I didn't. Not that I'm entirely certain I understand the real reason myself."

He paused, waiting for me to explain myself.

I, of course, couldn't get out a single word.

I'd never suffered such a long silence in the company of Denis before. He *always* started rambling to fill the silence.

But now he stayed silent. Staring at me from his spot against the door.

The only exit.

The silence couldn't have lasted more than two minutes but felt like hours. I started letting out a relieved breath when Denis finally broke it, then pulled it in again sharply once his words registered.

"You didn't actually steal the database, did you?"

"Of course I didn't!"

A slight frown appearing between his eyebrows, Denis' gaze stayed steady on my face. I couldn't bring myself to meet his eyes but stared at the door jamb to the right of Denis' head.

"You do realize your behavior seems highly suspicious with everything going on right now?"

I only managed a whisper and even then my voice shook. "You *know* that's not the reason."

He nodded. Once.

Leaning against the door, still except for his chest lifting with each breath. Face expressionless except for that tiny frown.

And another minute-long silence.

This time I was the one to break it. "I *know* I'm behaving weird, okay. But I'm freaking out. And you're right *there*. And I just—"

I had no idea how to finish that sentence. That was the problem. I didn't know what I wanted, what I felt, what I was doing.

I was completely lost.

Denis shifted from one foot to the other and finally dropped his gaze to the floor. "What if you could work from home the rest of the afternoon and tomorrow? Would that help?"

My eyes flew to his, but his gaze stayed on the floor. "You'd let me work from home?"

A glance up at me before turning away again. "I don't really have the power to do that but I think Tristan would go along with it if I ask him in the right way. But would it help? Will you be back on Monday?"

"I don't— Of course I— What will you tell him?" God, I hated the panic and whine in my voice. I *loathed* being like this. So weak and exposed.

At someone else's mercy.

I expected the look of a predator going in for the kill when Denis finally brought his gaze up from the floor. That's what I'd always seen in the past when I'd been in similar situations. People manipulate me to put me in a vulnerable situation then go in for the kill.

But Denis didn't attack. In fact, I was pretty sure that the tilt of his eyes and scrunching of eyebrows translated into pity.

I didn't want that either.

"I'll come up with something," he said, his voice calm and soothing like he was bringing a six-year-old down from a nightmare. "Tell him you have a family crisis or something and that you didn't want to tell him about it because you're really private."

He paused, staring into my eyes to make sure I was listening. "As long as you're back on Monday, it won't be a problem."

Not being able to stand the pity anymore, I bent my head and closed my eyes. I gave the world's smallest nod.

"Great." I heard Denis pushing off the door then opening it. "I'm available if you want to talk, okay?"

I nodded but we both knew that was never going to happen.

He held the door for me and I fled the room.

THIRTY-FOUR

Give Me the Juicy Details

SOMEHOW, I MANAGED to get work done from home that afternoon and the next day. I hardly slept, I drank a cup of herbal tea per hour without it having any calming effect whatsoever, and I chatted with Sylvie on Skype whenever I had a question.

At first, she wondered why I was asking her instead of Denis. Was helpful and told me Denis was right there, at his desk, totally available for any questions I might have.

> **Laure**: *I remember you talking about working on a bug kind of like this one a few weeks ago. Figured you'd know how to help.*
>
> **Sylvie**: *Well, sure, no problem. But I don't think it's exactly the same. And Denis is supposed to have a pretty good overview of everything.*

Laure: *Yeah, but I don't want to bother him all the time. He's spent so much time helping me already.*

Sylvie: *That's in his job description, you know. Just a second, I'll pop into his office to check if he has the time to help you out.*

Laure: *no*

Laure: *Please don't.*

Laure: *Sylvie? You still there?*

Sylvie: *Yeah…you're being weird. Weirder than usual. What's going on?*

I leaned my elbows on my desk and covered my face with my hands. I was breathing too fast. My heart galloped around in my chest like it had a five-headed flesh-eating monster on its heels. A drop of sweat trickled down my temple, sped down my neck, and ended up in the collar of my shirt.

God, I hated this.

I knew I was having a panic attack. I knew it was stupid. Sylvie wasn't going to make fun of me, or talk about me to our colleagues—at least not if I told her specifically not to.

I couldn't stand having someone know things about me that I hadn't planned or wanted them to know. My secrets were *mine*, and nobody else got to decide who was allowed to know.

I'd been burned before.

Never again.

I took a deep breath. Let it out—slowly.

One more. In. Out.

Come on, some rational thought. *I can do it.*

It wasn't the first time the bullying from eighth grade came back and influenced my adult life. It wasn't the first time I recognized my reaction as being out of proportion compared to what was going on.

But it was the first time I could lose my job over it.

And what for? Because a guy knew my secret.

A secret that I didn't want to get out.

My breathing sped up again.

"Dammit." I hit my fists against my forehead several times and growled in frustration. "This isn't like the eighth grade. It *isn't*. Denis isn't out to get me. Neither is Sylvie. Aaargh!"

My brain might know this wasn't like the time when my world had crumbled but my gut didn't agree.

I'd just have to ignore it.

This was *not* going to ruin my life. I might be able to live with being shy but not to the point of losing my job or my friends over it.

Laure: *I'm freaking out and it has to do with Denis.*

Sylvie: *Oh! Wow! Give me the juicy details :)*

Laure: *Please don't ask for any more information. I'm really freaking out here.*

Sylvie: *All right. No problem.*

Sylvie: *Still. You and Denis? I* knew *something was going on this weekend! Ha! Am I right?*

Sylvie: *Right. No questions. Sorry.*

Laure: *Can I please just ask you some questions about this bug I'm working on? And not tell anyone about any of this? Please?*

Sylvie: *Of course, Laure. I'm sorry I kept poking. Lay it on me.*

Sylvie kept her word. She helped me with the bug and promised, yet again, not to tell anyone.

When I logged off, I started berating myself for telling Sylvie that something had happened with Denis. For freaking out about telling her. For showing her how weird I was.

But I'd had it with all this panic. Those stupid girls from eighth grade were *not* going to ruin my life as an adult. Eighth grade was more than enough.

Deep breaths.

Logic.

Sylvie didn't judge me for going out with Denis. On the contrary, she seemed happy for me.

She promised not to tell the rest of the team—and I believed her.

She already thought I was weird before this whole thing. So what if I added one more point to the weirdo list?

I could *do* this. I was going to finish the tasks Tristan had set me for my days of working from home, and I was going back to the office on Monday and I'd face Denis with my head held high.

I'd avoid Denis but keep my head high.

Fuck it.

I was going back to the office on Monday.

Really.

THIRTY-FIVE

That's Chloé's Job

I SPENT MY Saturday writing. With my freaking out over Denis and my exposed secrets, I missed my usual Thursday chapter. All through Friday, the messages kept popping in from my regular readers, asking for the next chapter, wondering if I was okay.

I'd sort of decided that I'd miss that one post, for personal reasons, but when I saw the response from my readers it gave me the energy I needed to park my butt in my chair and get writing.

Denis wasn't the only one reading my stories. Even though it freaked me out that he would also read whatever I put out, I couldn't let that stop me from doing what I loved, and from sharing with my other online friends.

The bullying of my past was *not* going to ruin my writing.

So I read all the worried comments and messages from my readers—I skipped the one from DD—as a form of pep-talk, and then started writing.

As soon as the chapter was written, I posted it on the forum.

And got going with the next chapter. Because I knew myself well enough to realize I wouldn't be in great shape next week. I *was* going back to the office but it was going to take an enormous mental toll.

So I got the two chapters for Tuesday and Thursday ready, all proofread and queued up. Saying I was proud of myself would be something of an understatement.

I didn't read Denis/DD's Saturday chapter.

I got the notification when he posted it. I watched the number of comments and likes increase quickly as his readers came through. I hovered my mouse over the "Read now" link for what felt like hours—but I never clicked on it.

I knew—*knew*, he'd told me so less than two weeks ago—that this chapter had been written way before anything started up between us, before I freaked out on him. But I couldn't shake the fear that he'd somehow outed my secrets in his story, that people would read it and laugh at me.

That he'd betrayed my trust.

Even though I was one hundred percent sure he wouldn't do any of that, I preferred the doubt to the tiny possibility—less than zero percent according to my calculations but hey, panic sucks at math—that this was eighth grade all over again.

Sunday morning, I woke from fitful sleep, had a quick breakfast, and changed into my yoga pants to go over to Sabrina's.

I was looking forward to seeing my friends, even more than usual. If anyone could make me see sense, and remind me that there were people out there who cared about me, it was this group. They'd had my back since high school and had already seen me at my worst.

This wasn't going to chase them away.

I tapped on Sabrina's door five minutes early, a smile on my lips for the first time in days.

Sabrina opened, with a smile of her own—a forced one.

"What's wrong?" I asked her by way of greeting. I leaned in to do *la bise*, a hand on her shoulder as an additional way to show her I was here for her.

"Uh…" Sabrina greeted me in turn but her smile wobbled. "I might have done something stupid."

I chuckled. "You? Something stupid? Somehow, I doubt that. That's Chloé's job."

She let out a rapid breath that might have been intended as a laugh. "Right."

I took a step closer to move into the apartment, but Sabrina stayed put.

"Why are we still in the hall?" I asked.

"Right," she said again. She stepped aside and I walked in, toeing off my shoes as usual. I moved into the living room.

"I'm really sorry," Sabrina said from behind me.

There, leaning against the sliding doors leading to the balcony, was Denis.

"Morning, Laure. Imagine running into you here."

THIRTY-SIX

Take the Back Row and Enjoy the View

I WHIRLED AROUND to stare wide-eyed at Sabrina. "What's he doing here?" My fists were curled at my sides and I could hear my voice cracking on the last word.

"I'm so sorry," Sabrina repeated. She'd taken a step backward, her back hitting the closed front door, effectively blocking my exit. I could tell she was freaking out—the girl who was incapable of saying no, who wanted to please everyone and everything, the girl who hated having people's attention as much as I did—but I was too far gone in my own panic to be of any help in soothing her.

"It's not her fault," Denis said from behind me. Of course *he* had to step in and protect Sabrina. "I'm the one who contacted her on Facebook and barged in here uninvited. She only wanted to help."

"Help." My voice was flat as I turned—again, you'd think I was training to be a ballerina or something—meeting Denis' gaze across the room.

At least he hadn't moved. If he came closer to attempt *la bise* or *anything* requiring physical contact I was out. I didn't care if I had to manhandle Sabrina to get out the door. I was *not* letting Denis into my personal space.

Denis bit his lip and looked down at his feet. "You told me she was a bit of a pushover. So I pushed."

My eyebrows shot up and I looked around the room—only to discover for the first time that Chloé and Caroline were there, seated in two chairs pushed up against the far wall to make place for the yoga session.

My brain was running in panic in several directions at once but right now the anger was easier to deal with.

"You knew about this?" I asked my friends, pointing at Denis.

Caroline vehemently shook her head and Chloé held her hands up in surrender. "We discovered he was here when we arrived two minutes before you." She sent a mock glare at Denis. "Which was not enough time to grill him properly."

My heart attempted to jump out through my throat at the idea of Denis and my friends talking about me. Between the five of them, they knew *everything*. A squeak escaped before I could clamp my mouth shut. And I was fighting tears. Great.

"I wouldn't have told them anything, even after hours of grilling," Denis said. He kept his voice calm, probably in response to my obvious panic, but I could also hear a note of pleading. "I would never break your trust like that."

My eyes shot up to meet his. "And forcing your way in here isn't a breaking my trust?"

He swallowed. "We need to talk, Laure. And I don't think doing it in the office tomorrow would be ideal."

Well, he was right about that.

"I don't want to talk to you at all," I said. "Not today and not tomorrow."

"So you'll just play the ostrich and pretend nothing ever happened?"

"That's never going to work," Sabrina said from where she still stood plastered to the door. I was so surprised to hear her speak up in such a confrontational situation, I actually turned my head to check if she was okay.

"What?" she said, her eyes wide and voice squeaky. "It's true. If you don't talk it out with him, you'll end up quitting or getting fired. You're *not* going to be able to simply sweep this under the rug."

"I see your friends know you well," Denis said, and my head whipped back to face him. He still hadn't moved from his spot against the sliding doors. I suspected he was treating me like a wild animal, hoping I'd get used to his presence over time.

Fat chance.

"Talking to you in front of my friends isn't any better than doing it at the office."

"After yoga, then?" Caroline piped in, bouncing up from her seat and grabbing her yoga mat on the floor. When she saw my look of horror and incomprehension, she added, "You came here to work out and you clearly need it more than ever. Denis said he wanted to try it, too."

Denis smiled. "Somebody told me I should try it sometime. That I need to do more stretching. Not work out and skip the stretching like an idiot."

I narrowed my eyes at him. "You can find lots of yoga classes all over the city. Or install your own app. There's no need for you to barge in on our session."

"Actually," Chloé said as she unrolled her yoga mat next to Caroline's. "I'd love for him to stay. Since a certain someone won't tell us about what goes on in a certain online writers' forum, I figured 'DD' here could do it." She lifted her chin and gave a deceptively sweet smile at Denis.

Oh, no. No way. They were not getting information on my writing from Denis.

But before I could reply, Denis' reaction to Chloé's statement registered. He stood frozen in place, with a definite deer-in-headlights look to his brown eyes.

Ah. Hadn't he told Sabrina about his alter ego before forcing his way in here?

I felt a smile stretch across my lips.

I wasn't the only one with outed secrets. We'd see how he felt about being in the spotlight like that.

"I guess that sounds fair," I said, the challenge in my voice clear. "You get to do yoga with us, and in return you answer all these busybodies' questions about why you like to read and write romance and what your current WIP is all about."

The poor guy went white as a sheet and I think he had trouble remembering to breathe.

I'd feel bad—except I didn't.

"Now, I'd like to point out that I didn't tell the girls about the whole Denis-is-DD thing in order to tell them your secret. I did it because it freaked *me* out. And, you know, I was confident that they'd never meet you." When he still didn't move, I added, "Since you apparently think that people knowing that you write romance is no big deal, that's not a problem, right?"

Denis let out one long breath, then inhaled again.

"Sure," he said with a fake nonchalance that fooled no one. "No problem."

"All right then!" Chloé clapped her hands like we were a class of six-year-olds. "Sabrina, get Denis your extra mat." She grabbed Denis' elbow and led him to the spot right in front of the tablet with the yoga app. "You go here. Laure, you go to his left and Sabrina will take the right." She flashed a huge smile at Caroline. "Caroline and I will take the back row and enjoy the view."

I imagined Denis doing Down Dog with his ass in the air and couldn't stop the laugh at the idea of my friends ogling him.

Denis looked like he didn't understand what was so funny but was happy with me smiling.

"Fine," I said to nobody in particular. "I'll stay for yoga." I pointed a finger at Denis. "But I'm not having *the talk* in front of my friends."

Before lining up at the top of my mat when the app started up, I met my friends' gazes one by one. "Let the grilling begin."

THIRTY-SEVEN

What's the Word for Not Flexible?

"So what kind of romance do you write? Is it hot and steamy?"

"Laure told us your current work in progress has a character named Laure. Is she based on our Laure?"

"How do you go about writing the sex scenes? Do you do research?"

"You should do research with Laure!"

"You should do research with me! Ouch! That was a *joke*!"

"How did you get into writing romance?"

"Are you any good? Can I read your stories?"

The questions went on and on. They really did grill him, poor guy.

It gave *me* some time to get my bearings.

Denis hardly answered any of the questions. He had enough trouble breathing while following the yoga instructor on the tablet and he moaned and groaned every time he had to do a new pose. The Down Dog seemed to be particularly torturous for him. The angle of his pose was so wide he was close to just doing push-ups but he still complained about both his calves and his back.

"Seriously, dude," I told him as he grimaced his way through Cobra pose, of all things. I'd decided not to say anything while he was there but couldn't hold back any longer. "You need to stretch after playing soccer. It's not good for you to be so...what's the word for not flexible?"

"Soccer player," Caroline said from behind me.

That made Denis laugh and he mangled his Down Dog, managing to fall on his face into his mat.

I glanced up from my own pose, taking in the sprawled limbs and red face. "How is that even possible? Don't you have *any* balance?"

Denis rolled over to sit on his mat with his back to the app, facing the rest of us.

"Nah, hah," I told him. "No stopping. Just because you faceplanted does not give you an excuse to slack off. Get back up." I broke my Mountain pose and held out a hand to him to pull him up.

My classy friends let out a collective intake of breath when he fit his hand in mine.

I pulled Denis to his feet, then withdrew my hand as soon as I could. I stared daggers at my friends. "Shut it, guys. We're not your entertainment."

"Ah, but you are," Caroline said with a dreamy smile. None of the girls were following the instructions—the woman on the app was down in Cobra pose again and all of us were just standing around on our mats in Sabrina's living room.

"Seriously," Chloé told Denis. "I think you should do research with Laure. Can't write her sex scene without knowing what she likes. That'd be bad characterization."

How—but *how*—did she manage to say stuff like that with a straight face and not a speck of color on her fair skin?

My skin flamed so hard I was afraid my hair would catch on fire. Denis didn't fare much better and he didn't even have long hair to hide behind.

"Chloé!" I reprimanded her. "Shut it, will you?" I pointed to the tablet. "We're doing yoga. Let's get back to that."

"Fine," Chloé said as she flicked her hair over her shoulder like she was back in high school and slipped smoothly into the Warrior Two pose the instructor was telling us to do. "But doing yoga won't stop *me* from talking, you know. And we all know you want to jump each other, it's just a question of when you'll get over your hangups and relieve all this god-damned tension."

I couldn't look at Denis, had no idea how he reacted to that. I assumed the Warrior Two pose and focused *all* my attention on the woman on the screen.

Unfortunately, Denis' position right in front of the tablet meant that I couldn't get him entirely out of my field of vision, and when he wobbled his transition into Warrior Three, my eyes moved of their own accord.

He was *flaming* red, from his neck to the top of his shaved head.

Should I assume he *wanted* to "do research" with me? Gah, of course he did. I *knew* that. I *knew* he was interested, that he liked me. That wasn't the problem here.

The problem was that I hadn't been given the option of telling him my secrets. He'd gotten them out of me without my explicit consent and I didn't know if I trusted him with them.

The people who knew the most about me were the three girls in this room, and I'd known them for a decade or more. Little by little, I'd shared things with them, basically testing out their trustworthiness as we went. Caroline, I'd known since ninth grade. We hadn't been friends when I was shunned by everyone in school for the better part of eighth grade but she'd seen it happen. She knew why I had the scars that I had.

But even the girls didn't know everything. They knew I wrote stories, and they knew it was romance. But they'd never read any of it. We might get there one day—when I decided I was ready.

The girls knew that. It was why they kept pushing for it—because they knew it would be good for me. And because they wanted to know me better.

I'm sure it would have been possible for them to find my alias on that writers' forum if they'd wanted to. I wasn't hiding *that* well.

But they'd decided to respect my privacy.

I felt like Denis hadn't.

I'd shared things with DD that I hadn't shared with my closest friends, but under the protection of internet anonymity. Yes, I'd told a lot of things to DD, but I'd also held back a lot.

Like who I was. My name, my picture, my address, my job.

My real me.

I shared things in the logic that if DD judged me for anything, I could cut him out of my life. I could block him and move on. I'd never have to face him in real life, let alone every day at the office.

I felt violated.

As I balanced on my right foot with the left ankle resting on my right knee, I turned my head in Denis' direction. "We need to talk."

His balance had already been precarious. Now he whipped his head around to look at me and promptly fell over sideways.

He landed on his shoulders, legs in a jumble, his arms stuck under his body, and his face falling to a slow face-plant on the end of my mat.

"Talk is good," he said into the mat as he tried to get his limbs in place.

"Right!" Chloé said sharply, clapping her hands and walking up to stop the yoga app. "I think we'll cut today's session short." She shot an amused glance at Denis on the floor. "To avoid any further injury, yes?"

Meeting Caroline and Sabrina's eyes, she said, "Early lunch, girls? Sabrina, I'm sure you don't mind leaving your keys with Laure, do you? I think she could do with some privacy."

"Of course!" Sabrina ran straight to the front door, where she pulled her keychain off the door and shoved it into my hands. "Here. Just drop them in the mailbox when you leave. I have the key to that in my purse."

And before I could really get around to saying anything, or decide if I really was ready to *have a talk* with Denis, they were all out the door.

Denis hadn't even bothered to get up. He sat on his mat with his forearms leaning on his bent knees. I read both resignation, excitement, and anxiousness in his face.

"So." He swallowed audibly. "Ready to talk?"

THIRTY-EIGHT

So Much for Yoga Making You Mellow

We folded up the yoga mats and pulled Sabrina's table and chairs out from the wall, then sat down across from each other.

I was breathing heavily and my heart was tapdancing in my chest and it had nothing to do with the yoga. I couldn't meet Denis' eyes so I kept my gaze on an old coffee stain that Sabrina had never managed to get out of the grain of the wooden table no matter how hard she scrubbed.

"I'm angry at you for breaking my trust," I blurted out. I wanted to be the one to start the conversation and seeing how bad Denis was with silences, that meant I couldn't take the time to collect my thoughts.

Denis sighed. "So much for yoga making you mellow." He didn't really say it to me, it felt more like he was talking to himself.

I answered him anyway. "It did. I'm talking to you, aren't I?"

Another sigh. "I guess." He shifted on his seat. "I'm sorry, Laure. I know I messed up. I just—"

He placed his hand in my line of vision on the tabletop. "Hey. Won't you look at me while I'm apologizing?"

I stared at his hand. Observed how he chewed the nails of his thumb and forefinger but not the other three. Saw an ink stain on the back of his hand as if he'd written something on it and not gotten everything off when he cleaned it later.

I shook my head. "I can hear you just fine without looking at you."

"Fine." His voice shook a little and he cleared his throat before continuing.

"I was going to tell you, I swear," he said. His fingers started tracing along the lines of the wood on the tabletop. "At first, I only wanted to look at your stories on the forum, to see how your writing was and to see if our interests aligned at all. If they did, I was going to talk to you, tell you who I was."

"And then you didn't."

A pause. "I chickened out. We're both shy people and I guess I managed to convince myself that it was in everybody's best interest that we get to know each other on the forum anonymously. That it'd help us get closer. I really wanted us to get closer."

"Except it wasn't anonymous for you." My voice wasn't much more than a whisper but I was damned proud of myself for saying anything at all.

"I guess it wasn't," he agreed after a moment's silence. "But I swear I didn't hold anything back as DD when I chatted with you. It was just like if I'd met a perfect stranger online that I got along with really well."

"Because you still had the safety net of blocking me and never telling me who you really were."

More silence. A long one, this time. So long that I almost looked up to try to read his expression but I still couldn't do it. It took all my strength to stay in my chair and not run out the door to never be seen again.

"When did *you* figure out the connection?" Denis asked.

"The day we left for the weekend in the Pyrenees. Your phone kept pinging every time I sent a message to DD."

"Why didn't you say anything?"

I slammed my hand on the tabletop and finally lifted my angry gaze to meet Denis'. "Don't you *dare* compare that to you not saying anything."

Denis looked surprised at my outburst. His eyes were wide and he shot back in his chair so hard the chair scraped against the floor.

"I needed some time to process the fact that you and DD—who I'd been *convinced* was a girl and you never contradicted me—were one and the same person. I needed time to process the fact that *a colleague* knew a lot more about my personal life than I was comfortable with. I needed some time.

"You had months. You could give me a week."

Still pasted to the back of his chair, Denis seemed not to dare to move so much as a muscle in the face of my outburst. "I didn't—"

"Also," I continued, my voice rising. "Don't you dare compare our two situations. I happened to discover that a person I knew online and a person I knew in real life were in fact one. Then I needed some time to deal. *You* discovered that I was active on a forum that you also frequented and went out of your way to find my alias and get to know me as a stranger.

"Those two situations are *not* the same. You set out to lie from the get-go. You pretended to be a stranger. You let me believe you were a girl. You asked me lots of personal questions, all while knowing perfectly well who was on the other side of that conversation."

You hurt me.

As I finished my rant, I let my eyes fall back down to the tabletop. I'd managed to maintain eye contact while I laid into him but I couldn't keep it up while I waited for his reply.

He took his sweet time, too. For someone who didn't do well with silences, it was quite impressive.

"I'm sorry," he finally said, his voice hoarse. "I know I hurt you and I'm so, so sorry."

I risked a glance at his face. His expression agreed with his words. He looked genuinely sorry.

When I didn't say anything, he continued. "I don't really have an excuse for what I did. The explanation—*not* excuse, all right?—is that I'm as shy as you and scared of putting myself out there, and this gave me the possibility of testing the waters before doing that."

His eyes begged me to believe him. With his hair shaved off, those huge brown eyes were bloody hard to resist—but resist I did. I gave away nothing and waited for him to continue.

"Clearly, I got comfortable and waited too long." He ran a hand over his head, seemingly surprised to find the lack of hair. "I'll be perfectly honest and admit that if you hadn't figured it out yourself, it's quite possible that I would never have told you."

"But you wanted to date me," I said, fighting the blush that wanted to spread across my cheeks at what felt like fishing for compliments I didn't deserve. "Were you just looking for a quick fling? Because if not? If you were looking to start a relationship?

How did you plan on approaching the subject of reading and writing?"

I almost laughed at the irony of me throwing Sabrina's arguments at Denis, except I was too upset. I was even gesticulating with my hands as I talked, something I *never* did—it drew too much attention.

"Were you planning on never mentioning to me that you're also a writer? That you also read romance? Would this be some kind of dirty secret that you'd keep forever? What would you do the day I worked up the guts to tell you about *my* writing?"

Denis took a deep, ragged breath. "Clearly, I didn't think the whole thing through, Laure. And no, I wasn't planning on only having a fling with you. I meant what I said in those forum chats—I'm not into casual sex. I want serious. I want a real connection."

That was present tense, not past. He still wanted to go out with me.

Maybe.

Or I was reading too much into his choice of words in the heat of the moment.

"I still want you, Laure," he said in a voice so soft I could barely hear it. "You shouldn't doubt yourself so much. You're a wonderful girl and anyone would be lucky to have you."

God, I hated that he knew me well enough to know where my mind went when I felt insecure.

Normally, I wouldn't give any more information about myself in this situation. I'd keep my cards close to my chest and hide myself and my emotions as best I could.

But I knew where that reflex came from. From that damned eighth grade and those stupid people who got into my head even ten plus years later.

And that was *not cool.*

So I forced the words out, despite my heart beating fast and my stomach doing somersaults. "I know that up here," I said, tapping a finger to my temple. "It's easy to logically come to the conclusion that someone could find me attractive. That someone could want me. But in here," and I pointed to the center of my chest, the part that felt like a nuclear reaction was about to go off, "I *don't* know it. I *can't* believe it."

I drew in some air—not enough but the best I could do under the current circumstances. "And that's the part that's going to win out every time."

I felt like Denis' gaze went right into my soul. "Because of that stuff that happened to you when you were fourteen, right?"

Because I'd told DD about that, of course.

"Yes."

Denis nodded, his eyes taking on a distant look. "My aunt's first husband was a real piece of work. Abusive."

Nice subject change. I had no idea how to respond. So I didn't.

"She had flashbacks and weird reactions to the oddest stuff because of him, even years after the divorce." He visibly braced himself for my reaction as he went on. "Eventually, somebody convinced her to go see a psychologist. And after a year of some pretty hard work on her part, she was finally able to put her past behind her for good."

I sat stock still. To the point where I apparently stopped breathing and started seeing stars.

"This is how you see me?" I finally ground out in a broken whisper.

"How I see you?" Denis shook his head with a sad tilt to his eyes. "You think because I tell you it'd be a good idea to see a psychologist, I think you're crazy? That's the conclusion you're coming to?"

Of course it was. I stared back at him.

"Psychology isn't for 'crazy' people, Laure. It's for everyone. It's for helping you work through your own problems. Hell, *I* went to see one on the regular for two years after my parents split up."

Oh, yeah, he'd told me about that on the forum.

"It can help you get past the shit that's bogging you down, Laure. Help you get back to living your life."

"So you think that if I get past 'my shit,' then I'll be acceptable to go out with?"

"What?" Denis moved for the first time in ages, leaning forward, toward me. "What the hell are you— You *do* realize you're putting words in my mouth, here? Words I would *never* say."

My teeth ground together so hard I had a weird and awful sound resonate through my head. My eyebrows drew together as I searched for the falseness in Denis' words.

"I would go out with you *this minute*," Denis almost yelled, his arms thrown out for emphasis. "You're a great and wonderful girl, Laure, and I love you. I don't suggest you get help for *me*, so that I can get some sort of perfect girlfriend—whatever the hell that means!—I'm doing it *for you*. It would help you *so much* if you could get those girls' voices out of your head."

My mouth hung open. The only sound coming out was of the air exiting my lungs, making me sound like a deflated tire.

"What?" Denis said, clearly worried as his gaze traveled across my face, over my torso, to my eyes. "What's wrong? What did I say wrong now, to set you off?"

God, he didn't even realize he'd said it?

Did that mean that it was *that* obvious to him? Or that it was a throwaway phrase of sorts and he didn't really mean it?

Did I *have to* over-analyze *everything*?

I took a deep breath in the hope it would be enough to get a few words out. "You…you love me?" My voice squeaked on the word *love*, of course, and my face was so hot I might need moisturizer after—but I got the words out.

Yay, me.

Denis froze. "Uh…" His eyes darted left and right as I could *see* him trying to remember what he'd said. "I said that, huh?"

I nodded.

He deflated. His face flamed red. As he took a deep breath, his entire body shook.

"Well, it's true, Laure." He met my eyes across the table, making sure I could see he was being completely honest. "I do love you. See, another advantage of knowing you were Lily was that I got to know both sides of you. And they're both wonderful."

"But…" My head was spinning. I was having the worst time keeping up. "But the Laure in your story. She's so much prettier. And funnier. That isn't *me*. You see this…idealized version of me. *That's* who you love."

"Oh, for crying out loud." Denis shoved his chair back and stood up.

He was leaving.

I'd shown yet another weakness and now he was giving up on me.

He stepped around the table and pulled me up by my shoulders until I was standing in front of him, basically leaning on his chest because my legs weren't working all that well.

"The Laure in my story is based one hundred percent on *you*," he said, with one hand holding onto my chin to force me to look at him. "*You're* beautiful. *You're* funny. You're perfect—for me."

And he leaned in and kissed me.

THIRTY-NINE

Good Etiquette

His scent enveloped me completely. He smelled of aftershave, and fresh sweat, and Denis.

His lips were soft against mine, not really moving, but pushing tenderly as if ready to do more if I gave some sort of green light. His hand on my chin moved in a soft caress toward my neck, his fingers sliding through the hair around my ear. His other hand found its way to my lower back.

I could have gotten out of his embrace if I wanted to. He clearly took great pains to hold me without actually *holding* me. He knew I was a flight risk and wasn't sure about the reception his kiss would get.

It was this uncertainty that finally got me moving, got me out of my own head.

I wasn't the only nervous one, the only one who felt exposed. Although Denis had taken a lot of initiative in our relationship these last days, I knew him well enough to know it must have taken a lot out of him to do it.

He was almost as shy as I was.

And yet, here he was, forcing his way into a yoga session, making love declarations to someone doing her best to push him away, and kissing her to make a point.

I realized I could feel his heart beating—fast—where I'd placed my hand on his chest. His breathing was quick, as if he'd been running.

His lips left mine. His hands stayed in place.

I hadn't kissed him back. Except for the hand now on his chest, I hadn't moved at all since the kiss started.

All because of my damned shyness.

Which was unacceptable.

Shoving away all the warning bells in my mind and the fear creeping up my spine, I went up on my toes and kissed Denis.

I wanted this and I wasn't going to let the stupid fear let it slip away.

Denis didn't take long to respond. The hand on my back pulled me closer, bringing my body flush up against his, letting me feel the heat of him on my chest, against my hips. He kissed me back with fervor, letting out something between a groan and a sigh when our tongues touched for the first time.

Everything else blurred into the background as the kiss took over for all conscious thought. Denis' lips moved slowly against mine, tongue darting out to run along my lips or to smooth against my tongue.

I felt warm and protected and loved.

My right hand stayed on Denis' chest, enjoying the feel of his heart beating for me, and the heat of his skin through his t-shirt.

My other hand stayed immobile by my side at first, but little by little, dared to participate and do some exploring.

Its first stop was Denis' back. My hand slipped under his arm and traced along Denis' spine, starting at his neck and finishing at the waistline of his shorts.

When the result was Denis pulling me even closer and sucking even harder on my tongue, I took that as an invitation to continue.

I did the same movement, but under the t-shirt this time.

His skin was warm and slightly sticky under my hand. I traced every vertebrae in his back with my index finger as I traveled south and felt slight bumps with my other fingers, either from beauty marks or possibly mosquito bites.

Again, I stopped at the shorts. I kept my hand there, enjoying the skin on skin, running my little finger along the rugged waistline.

I realized I wanted to put my hand down the back of his shorts. I wanted to pull the damned things off.

I tore away from the kiss as the realization hit me.

I want to sleep with him.

It was way too soon for that.

We'd only just gotten together and I was ready to take him to bed? What had gotten into me? Had I taken a leaf out of the book of one of my characters?

I remembered what Denis told me in our chat: *I happen to prefer for the feelz to be in place before they actually jump in the sack.* And he'd confirmed that was how he worked in real life too.

I wasn't about to force myself on the poor guy.

I removed my hand from his back.

"What's wrong?" Denis said, his eyes wide and cheeks flushed. His eyes searched mine, jumping from the left to the right and back again.

"I don't—" I put a hand to my barrette, noticing it had miraculously stayed in place during our makeout session. "I know you don't want to—"

Yeah, no, not figuring out how to say that.

"I don't want to what?" Denis was rather breathless and although his hand stayed on my back, I could feel him tensing up. "Keep kissing me? Putting your hand down my shorts?"

His face turned *flaming* red at that last part but he maintained eye contact.

My face couldn't have been much better, faced with being caught quite literally redhanded.

I couldn't draw breath, let alone utter any words.

"I'd love for you to do both of those. For the record."

"But you don't—" I closed my eyes and consciously drew a deep breath. I needed air in order to get words out. "You don't believe in jumping into the sack straight away," I finally forced out, talking very fast.

He blinked at me. Stood stock still and just looked at me while he blinked, like he was trying to do a reset of his brain and it didn't work.

"Straight away." His voice was completely flat. "We've been flirting on and off for months. *I* have known that I was flirting with you online as well as in real life. I've been in love with you since way before we even had our first kiss."

It looked like he was fighting off a smile and his voice became forced. "And you think this is *too soon*?"

I got stuck on the love declaration again.

He'd said *several times* that he loved me. Could it actually be true?

"Laure?" Denis bent down to put himself in my line of sight where I'd zoned out while staring at his chest. "You still with me?"

I met his eyes and nodded. Swallowed.

"Is it too soon for *you*?" he asked gently.

I shook my head.

"You sure?"

Fervent nodding.

Denis chuckled. It was warm and cozy and sexy, all in one. I'd love to bask in his laugh for hours.

He turned to look toward Sabrina's bedroom. "I'm not sure if it's really good etiquette to have sex in your host's bedroom."

I burst out giggling. Denis had to step away as I bent in half laughing, my mirth and stress bubbling out in laugh after laugh, giggle after giggle. At one point I thought I was done but then the sight of Denis standing awkwardly in my friend's living room sent me off in another fit.

"Right," Denis said with a huge smile across his handsome face when I managed two consecutive breaths without laughing. "Your place or mine?"

FORTY

Don't Move

We decided on my place. It was the closest to our current location and I felt a little safer doing it in my home rather than a room I'd never seen. We both took our separate cars and Denis followed me closely through the streets of Toulouse.

As I stood in front of my apartment door, with Denis breathing down my back—quite literally; he leaned into my back with one hand on my hip and his lips grazing the skin on the back of my neck—my heart beat wildly in my chest and my hands shook as I tried to fit the key into the lock.

"You know we don't have to, right?" Denis mumbled and placed a tiny kiss at the junction of my neck and my shoulder. "We can just make out or something if that's what you prefer." Another tiny kiss. "Or talk."

I drew a ragged breath. "We do need to talk some more." The door finally opened and I threw my bag inside, not caring where it landed. The clang that rang out probably meant I'd hit the umbrella rack that hadn't seen an umbrella in years, but I didn't care.

I turned in Denis' arms, grabbed onto the front of his t-shirt with one hand. "But we'll do that later," I said firmly, feeling giddy at the confidence in my own voice. "Right now, creating sentences might be asking too much of my brain."

I put my second hand on the back of his neck and pulled him in for a kiss.

We stumbled into the apartment together and somehow we managed to close the door and kick off our shoes without ever breaking the kiss.

I pulled Denis with me toward my bed, hands wandering all across his body and my body lighting up wherever he touched me.

I especially liked it when he cradled my face while he kissed me.

Made me feel seen.

The back of my knees bumped into my bed. Without even stopping to think about what I was doing, and without a flicker of a doubt, I grabbed the bottom of Denis' t-shirt and pulled it up over his head.

We had to break the kiss in order to get rid of the t-shirt. Once his head popped out, our eyes met for a second and we both broke out in huge grins before fusing our lips together yet again.

My hands started exploring, making sweeps across Denis' chest, mapping it out. He didn't have very defined muscles—typical soccer player all around—but he was very solid and warm with a smattering of hair in the middle of his chest.

I explored a little farther down—ah, the infamous happy trail.

Denis blew something that must have been a laugh out of his nose. Because it tickled or because he had the same thought as me?

We separated so that our eyes could meet. Neither of us said a word but yeah, he'd had the same thought as me, flashing to countless sex scenes in various stories, suddenly something real.

Denis took the opportunity to get rid of my t-shirt. He had to remove my barrette first and he carefully unlatched it before placing it gently on my nightstand. The bra followed—not particularly elegantly since, by definition, a sports bra is supposed to be tight.

It wasn't awkward, though. We laughed about it together and both let out a sigh of relief when the bra went flying to the corner and Denis let one hand drop to my breast.

That's nice.

Seriously, skin on skin really was something.

I tilted my head to the side and closed my eyes to focus only on the feeling of Denis' hand moving slowly across my skin, grazing his thumb over my nipple and giving the breast a gentle squeeze.

His other hand joined in the fun and gave the other breast the same treatment.

I realized I was just standing there, letting Denis do all the work. That wouldn't do.

More skin sounded like a good plan. So I brought my hand to the small of Denis' back, where it had been earlier while we were in Sabrina's living room, with my finger grazing the top of his shorts.

I lingered there for a moment, to enjoy the feeling of his skin and the dip of his spine, but also to make sure he really didn't mind.

When he didn't say anything but lowered his head to suck on my neck, I took that as a green light. I curled the fingers of both hands into the waistline of Denis' shorts and slowly pushed them and his boxers down over his hips.

A part of my brain couldn't believe what I was doing. This was *Denis* who stood naked in front of me in my own apartment. *Denis* who moaned as his quite interested dick came into contact with my still-clothed hip, and he sucked all the harder on my neck.

That was probably going to leave a mark and I couldn't care less.

What I *did* care about was that last piece of clothing. I grabbed one of Denis' hands and guided it to the top of my yoga pants.

It didn't take him long to take the hint. With one hand still exploring my breast, the other pushed down my pants and underwear, a little on one side then the other, to get everything over my hips and finally pool at my feet.

I was extremely aware of the air caressing my exposed skin, of how close Denis' hand was to my ass…to everything.

My own hands had, of course, taken the opportunity to explore Denis' derriere. It was firm, hairy, and a great place to grab onto. As he shifted, his muscles moved under my hands and I couldn't wait to learn what it would feel like when he used those muscles to push into me.

In order to get that to happen as soon as possible, I detached my mouth from Denis for a quick second. "I need to go to the bathroom to get a condom," I said, my gaze locked on Denis' mouth and the way it looked thoroughly kissed. *I'd* done that.

"Uh…" Denis shook his head a little, as if working hard to make sense of my words. Then something connected and he jumped into action, bending down to grab his discarded pants. "I got one right here."

I couldn't help a bark of laughter from escaping. "Came prepared, didn't you?"

His smile was both sheepish and wolfish. "A man can dream."

We wasted no time. I jumped onto the bed and scooted back to make room for Denis. He looked like nothing less than a god as a beam of sunshine from outside hit him when he crawled on all fours toward me across my bedding, highlighting the muscles of his thighs and making the hairs on his chest gleam almost golden.

He paused to put on the condom. I had flashbacks to innumerable stories where the hero rips the package with his teeth and puts in on one-handed.

Denis must have had the same thought. "I'm not risking ripping it with my teeth," he said while flashing a huge smile. "And I'm afraid I'm not quite experienced enough to do this with one hand and without looking."

"Disappointing," I said, making it clear with my expression that it was anything but.

I was utterly charmed.

"Wanna help?" He held out the unpacked condom, his eyes warm with laughter and something that might be that love he kept talking about.

My hand lifted of its own accord, slowly, taking the little piece of rubber.

Denis scooted closer, nudged my legs open with his knees, and placed his feet on either side of my hips.

We were both in very open and exposed positions—but I didn't feel even the beginnings of shyness or shame.

This was why you waited to jump into bed until the feelz were in place. I trusted him not to do anything I wouldn't like and *knew* he wouldn't make fun of me or hurt me in any way, physical or otherwise.

Clearly, Denis felt the same way. He didn't seem shy about how his dick jutted out between us, reaching toward me, impatient to be covered in its plastic cape so that the fun could begin.

I met Denis' gaze. "I've never done this before," I said and brought the condom closer to my eyes so I could figure out which way was up. I found the direction it was rolled in and squeezed the top together.

"Looks like you know what you're doing," Denis said and guided my hand to his dick.

"I read a lot," I said, my voice almost giving out because I was so excited. Then I giggled.

"See," Denis whispered back, "that's why it's a good idea to go out with a bookworm." He hissed out a breath as I made contact.

I held the condom over the tip with one hand and gently rolled it down with the other while Denis gritted his teeth and breathed heavily.

I was pretty sure it wasn't because he was in pain.

When he was finally sheathed our eyes lifted from where we'd both watched the proceedings to stare at each other. Denis' pupils were so blown I could hardly tell the actual color of his eyes and I had no doubt mine were much the same. His entire torso was flushed and the color in his cheeks made him look more alive than I'd ever seen him.

"You're gorgeous," I blurted out, then widened my eyes and slapped a hand over my mouth. How embarrassing.

Denis smiled serenely. "Hey." He pulled my hand away from my mouth and held it in his. "*Thank you*. I'm flattered." He ran a light caress down the side of my face with his free hand, the knuckles of his fingers barely grazing my cheekbones. "Feel free to give me compliments anytime."

I let out a relieved breath. "I'm nervous."

"Me, too," Denis said, his eyes studying every part of my face. "We can stop whenever if you don't want to continue, okay?"

I nodded. "I don't want to stop, though. I'm just nervous."

He chuckled. "Okay. You're gorgeous, too, by the way. I can't believe I'm finally allowed to touch you."

"Please don't hold back on the touching," I said on a sigh.

My first reflex was to try to take the statement back again because it was putting myself out there too much, but I fought it back. I squeezed Denis' hand and placed my other hand on his chest.

That chest hair really was fascinating.

I ran my fingers through it, scraping along his skin with my nails. I enjoyed the mix of soft skin and rough hair, and the masculine strength underneath.

Denis placed my other hand on his chest with a smile and brought both of his hands to my face, pulling me in for a scorching kiss.

I expected things to happen quickly. He was already suited up, after all, and I was more than ready.

But Denis had decided to take things slow. The kiss went on forever, to a point where I forgot where we were, what had happened with my friends earlier, what would happen at work tomorrow. All I could feel were Denis' lips on mine, his tongue against mine, and his hands roving over my body.

Little by little, we ended up horizontal, with Denis on top of me. As he settled in between my legs, I spread them wide, inviting him in, enjoying the slight rush of air over my glistening sex, reminding me that I was utterly naked and ready for the next step.

"Still don't want to stop?" Denis whispered in my ear as the tip of his dick touched on my entrance.

"God, no," I practically moaned. I ran a hand over his shaved head, feeling the tickles of the hair starting to grow back, and pulled him down by the neck so he could kiss my shoulder. I arched my back so that I could feel his dick against me, so that I could speed him up.

The tip was basically already inside and we both hitched a breath at the feeling. I felt the beginnings of that delicious stretch and lowered my hands to his ass so I could pull him against me and get him *in* already.

Denis let out a relieved groan and pushed inside.

I threw back my head and reveled in the dual feeling of the muscles of his ass clenching in my hands and his dick sliding home to the hilt, the heat of him stretching me and making me hyper aware of our connection.

I winced a little at the stretch—I hadn't done this often, and that was quite a few years ago.

"You all right?" Denis asked, his face too close for me to really see the details of his features but I could see the worry line between his eyebrows just fine.

"I'll be fine," I replied, making sure to smile since my voice was kind of breathless. "I need a minute to adjust. Just…don't move, okay?"

I felt a puff of air on my chin. Then heard a snort as Denis' body jerked a little bit.

"I think that's kind of the point," he said, having more and more trouble keeping the laughter back. "You know…moving?"

I burst out laughing—which felt downright weird with him inside me like that. But the fact that we were joking and bantering also made me relax and suddenly that little sting that had made me call a timeout was gone.

I brought a hand to his chin and lifted it up to place a kiss on his nose. "You can move now. Show me what you got."

And he did.

FORTY-ONE

Sex Was Even Better Than Yoga

I WAS ON cloud nine as I lay cradled in Denis' arms. I felt exhausted and exulted and completely mellow.

Sex was even better than yoga for relaxing.

A few rays of afternoon sunlight slanted through a gap in my curtains and made it look like God himself was giving us his blessing.

God, I was sappy. I had to make sure none of this crap made its way out of my mouth or Denis would never let me live it down. He *hated* purple prose.

I glanced up at him, where he seemed to also be lost in thought and gazing at the sunlight while his hand traced lazy circles on my shoulder.

It seemed like my brain had finally managed to merge Denis and DD. I didn't have to do a mental hop in order to think of things that DD had told me online. I thought of them as Denis' opinions.

This meant that one single person knew a lot of personal information about me. Things that could become hurtful if they were used as ammunition in the right context. I knew, intellectually, that I shouldn't care about what others thought of me, but my gut was far from catching on.

I *did not* want anyone at work to know about my writing.

But as I lay there, naked in bed with Denis, I realized I trusted him. He wouldn't tell them about the writing. He wouldn't show them my stories. And—

"I'm not sure if I want our colleagues to know about us," I said, one finger trailing along Denis' collarbone.

He turned his head to look at me. In this light, I realized that his brown eyes were far from being only brown. There was a whole lot of green in there, and even some flecks of golden yellow.

"That's okay," he said. "You can decide if and when we tell them." He squeezed my shoulder. "Just don't go around behaving like a criminal and make Tristan wonder if you're a security risk."

I growled in frustration and tried to hide my face in Denis' chest. I wasn't very successful, but it was nice. "God, I'm so sorry about that. I was totally freaking out."

"Yeah, I could tell," Denis said. He sighed. "We might need to tell him *something* to get him off your back, though. He was genuinely concerned that you might have been behind the data theft they discovered earlier this week."

"Yeah. Fair enough." I drew a deep breath. "I'll talk to him on Monday. Do you think if I tell him, he'll keep the secret from the rest of the team?"

"He'll probably tell Fidi but I have no doubt he'll keep silent about it to the rest of the guys. I mean, we need to tell him *something* because he thinks your weird behavior has to do with work. But once he learns it's something personal, he'll back off—and there's absolutely no reason to tell everyone else."

We lay there in silence for several minutes. It was a comfortable silence but I could tell Denis had something on his mind. I waited for him to come out with it.

"I'm sorry I manipulated your friend to barge in on your Sunday yoga," he finally said, his gaze on the ceiling. "That was totally out of character for me but I was getting desperate."

I continued trailing my finger along his collarbone, my eyes on what I was doing and not on the guy I was talking to. "It's all right. I mean, don't get me wrong, I was *not* happy to see you there. And I'm kind of creeped out about how you must have stalked me to even get into contact with Sabrina."

"Through Facebook," he mumbled. "I remembered you talking about her and how she was a pushover, so I went through your list of friends on Facebook and found only one Sabrina."

"Right." I chewed the inside of my cheek. "Like I said. Creepy."

"Sorry."

"Still." I sighed. "I have no idea how Monday would have gone if you hadn't showed up today. There's absolutely no guarantee that I'd have managed to behave normally. There's a good chance you just saved my job."

He gave me a one-armed squeeze. "I wouldn't have let it come to you losing your job. If necessary, I might have told Tristan the truth and asked him not to tell you he knew."

I pulled up so I could see him and so he could see how angry I was. "That's so sneaky! And deceitful."

That was definitely pity I saw in his eyes. "And I still would have done it if it was the only way to convince Tristan you weren't a thief or a complete lunatic."

"Gee, thanks."

"What you don't know can't hurt you, right? And I *didn't* have to do it."

"Right." I threw myself back down on the pillow and hid my face in my hands. "Because now *I* have to do it."

"If it freaks you out that much, you don't *have to* do it."

"Yes, I do." I sighed and let my hands fall to my chest. "I have to do it *because* it freaks me out that much. I'm sick and tired of this crap ruining my life."

Silence stretched out between us but it wasn't uncomfortable. We were both lost in our thoughts.

I went back to the conversation we'd had earlier, when Denis suggested I go see a therapist. We'd been derailed because he'd slipped that love declaration in there, too, but he'd made his point come across.

Could it be worth it, to get those girls' taunting out of my head? Was it possible?

Eyes on the ceiling, I whispered, "You wouldn't happen to know of a good therapist around here?"

I could feel Denis turning his head but couldn't bring myself to look at him. "As a matter of fact, I do," he said. "I'll send you the name, address and phone number as soon as I get my hands on my phone."

"Thank you." My heart was speeding but I also felt my mind calming down. It felt good to have made the decision.

"So are we okay?" Denis asked, pushing himself up on one elbow so he came into my field of vision. "You're not angry for me manipulating Sabrina? Or for not telling you earlier that I was DD?"

I narrowed my eyes and met his gaze. "I'm not happy about either of those things. But I'm thinking we can get past it."

Denis visibly deflated and closed his eyes in relief.

"Just don't ever do something so sneaky ever again."

Denis nodded vigorously. "I promise. Now." He perked up and looked around my room, searching. "Where's your computer?"

"Huh? What do you need that for?" As if I'd ever let anyone else use my computer. I might be in love with this guy, but that would seriously be pushing it.

"*I* don't need it," he said with a huge grin. "But you still haven't read my last chapter. You have some catching up to do."

I couldn't have stopped the smile from stretching across my face if I'd wanted to. He'd noticed that I hadn't commented on his story. We'd traded comments of this style back and forth online before—between Lily and DD—but we'd never done it in person.

It was *nice*. He wanted my feedback.

"Is there a sex scene?" I asked him with a wink.

Denis waggled his eyebrows. "Guess you'll have to read it and see."

Damn him.

I jumped out of bed and went to get my laptop from the desk.

FORTY-TWO

Don't Mind Me

READING DENIS' WRITING with Denis—naked Denis!—watching me was quite the experience.

I attempted to put on my underwear on my way to get my laptop but Denis stopped me, told me to leave it where we'd thrown it earlier. I felt a little self-conscious at walking around in front of him stark naked but I also felt sexier than I'd ever felt before with the way his eyes ate me up from his spot on the bed.

I settled in against my headboard, my sheets covering my lap and my laptop firing up.

Denis lay next to me, his head propped on a pillow so it was on a level with my breasts and his hand on my thigh under the sheets, squeezing lightly.

I clicked my way to Denis' latest chapter and started reading.

The first time I laughed, Denis' head popped up so he could look at the screen. At first I thought he was annoyed that I'd laughed in the wrong place or something but then my inner writer kicked in.

All writers love feedback. Positive feedback is great, but even criticism can be good, so long as it's done in a constructive way. It's not always easy, however, to understand *why* someone loved one chapter and hated another when their feedback is three words and a bunch of emojis.

Denis was watching me read his story live, with the possibility of checking out exactly which line made me react.

I was totally having him read my next chapters in front of me.

But right now, it was his turn. Fred and Laure were at it again, the sexual tension through the roof and their banter funny and smart.

It was kind of distracting to have Denis there, staring up at my face from his pillow, clearly searching out any and all reactions. But the story drew me in quickly and after a while, I completely forgot Denis was even there.

Until the sex scene.

I'd been complaining about him postponing the first sex scene for weeks, and now, the one time he was *right there*, watching me read, Laure and Fred's clothes went flying.

And it was hot. Of course it was hot.

I shifted on the bed, spreading my legs a little, pushing against the sheets.

I felt Denis move his head a little—probably to check where I was in the chapter—and then his hand moved farther up my thigh.

My breath caught and I sent him a look that was supposed to be accusatory but was probably somewhere between deer-in-the-headlights and turned-on-like-never-before.

"Keep reading," Denis murmured, his hand sliding slowly up and down the inside of my thigh, every time going a little higher. "Don't mind me."

I almost choked on my laughter but went back to reading.

And spread my legs a little wider.

Denis jumped on the invitation. With a glance at the screen to see where I was in the story, he disappeared under the sheets and crawled over my leg to settle in the space I'd created for him.

I lifted my knees so he could fit his arms underneath and when I felt the stubble of his beard scratch along my inner thigh, I let out a sigh that ended on a whimper.

I kept reading. It might seem impolite to do so while Denis' mouth hovered so close to my sex I could feel his warm breath, but I *knew* this guy. I knew he loved writing and stories—and stories about romance most of all. He *wanted* me to read his words while he went down on me. He *wanted* to get to me both physically and mentally.

I knew because that's how I would feel—and couldn't wait to reciprocate.

So I lay in a horribly uncomfortable position, with my laptop on my stomach and Denis between my legs, and I read.

And Denis must have been a psychic or something because the moment Fred laid hands on Laure's body in the story, his tongue started kissing my thighs. First one side, then the other, every kiss a little higher than the last one.

When Fred started fondling story-Laure's breasts, Denis reached his destination and gave a long, decadent, thorough lick.

"Holy shit!" I exclaimed and almost dropped the laptop on the floor. The fact that I almost didn't care said quite a bit about Denis' prowess.

It all escalated from there. Fred and Laure in the story had the most epic sex scene ever and Denis started licking and sucking like a pro.

I writhed and moaned and pushed against him to get him to go deeper, faster, stronger. I somehow managed to also keep reading because the dual inputs were *such* a turn-on.

My entire body vibrated with need and my breathing grew ragged.

Denis moaned right along with me, creating delicious vibrations to go with his dangerously talented tongue.

I was getting close, so close.

I had increasing trouble with keeping my eyes open to keep reading but luckily I could see the end was near. So I forced my eyes to cooperate for the last three paragraphs, accompanying story-Laure in her climax.

Finally allowing myself to close my eyes, I threw my head back and screamed out my orgasm while my last brain cell pushed the laptop off onto the mattress beside me so it wouldn't end up broken on the floor.

Denis wound down his ministrations and pulled down the sheet, probably so he could breathe properly.

I put my hand on his shaved head and focused on getting my breathing back, skin tingling and brain shutting down.

When he spoke, Denis' voice was hoarse and gravelly. "So. Can I assume you liked the chapter?"

FORTY-THREE

Under the Influence

DENIS SPENT THE night. He nudged me awake at six in the morning to ask if I wanted him to go home before work so that we'd arrive in separate cars. Groggy and under the influence of his strong, male naked body, I told him to stay.

In the bright light of eight o'clock in what passed for a kitchen in my apartment, I started having second thoughts.

I wasn't used to having someone in my space during my morning routine. My hair was all over the place, I probably had morning breath, and I wasn't wearing a barrette.

That last bit bothered me more than it should and I kept touching my hair where the barrettes usually were.

Denis noticed, of course, and started running his hand through my hair while we stood leaning against my kitchen sink side by side since I didn't have a kitchen table. I usually took my breakfast curled up in my comfy chair.

"You have lovely hair," he said as he pulled on a strand.

I gave him a flat stare. "It looks like a bird decided it was a good place to make a home. It's so tangled it's going to take me twenty minutes to brush it after I shower and I'm pretty sure it's stuck to my head on the side where I slept on your chest."

I blushed a little but managed to ignore it.

Denis smiled serenely, his eyes on half-mast as he ran his fingers through my hair yet again. "It's lovely."

Okay, fine, I probably *could* get used to this.

We finished our coffees and cereals and took our turns at the shower. While it was Denis' turn, I stood in front of my bathroom mirror, with the door to the bathroom cabinet containing my barrettes open, staring at the rows of fake flowers.

I did wear them because they were pretty and because I enjoyed looking at them. The colors, the textures, the reminder of the beauty of nature.

But I also wore them to avoid direct eye contact. They drew people's attention away from my face and that helped me relax. I noticed it, too. People would talk to me and their eyes would wander a little bit to the side, drawn to the bright colors. It meant I wasn't the one to break eye contact and I didn't feel like I was under a lens all the time, continually judged.

I couldn't believe I was *just* coming to realize that I feared people's judgment pretty much all the time.

That probably wasn't normal.

If there even was such a thing as "normal," of course.

Still, it *was* something that stopped me from being myself, and was probably holding me back at work.

And I was going to get *rid* of it, dammit.

I eyed the silhouette of Denis behind my shower curtain, then the barrettes.

I'd try not wearing a barrette tomorrow. That wasn't procrastinating, simply not doing everything at once, so as to give my heart a living chance.

Today I had another scary thing to do.

FORTY-FOUR

I'd Love to Do It Tonight

IN OUR COMPANY's parking lot, I stepped out of Denis' car with the feeling of having hundreds of eyes on me.

Looking around, I only saw empty cars, of course, but the feeling remained. There *could* be people at the windows, surveying the parking lot, looking for juicy gossip.

I inwardly rolled my eyes at myself at the level of unrealistic drama my brain was able to come up with.

"So I tried that book you told me about," Denis said conversationally as we walked toward the main entrance, not holding hands, not walking too close. We'd carpooled, that's all. Nothing to see here.

"What book?" I was pretty sure I'd seen movement in a window on the third floor. Or it could have been the reflection of a bird.

"The one from that new author you told me about. The M/M one?"

That got my attention.

I whirled around to look at him and tripped over my own feet on the perfectly smooth ramp leading up to the doors.

Denis caught my elbow, keeping me from falling on my face, but let go and stepped away as soon as I had my feet under me. His smug half-smile told me he'd done this on purpose, to get my mind off the stuff that was stressing me out.

"And?" I asked him. I stopped, right there on the path, because I wanted to see his face when he replied and I didn't want to fall again.

"And…" Denis shoved his hands down the front pockets of his jeans, making his shoulders ride up in a shrug. "So far, it's good."

"So far," I repeated. "How much have you read?"

A one-shoulder shrug, a smile, and the beginnings of a blush. "I'm about halfway through."

Which meant there'd been at least one sex scene already.

"It's good?" I said, repeating his words as a question rather than agreeing with him.

"Mm-hmm." He was blushing pretty strongly now but his gaze stayed on mine and his smile kept growing.

I let out a breathless laugh. "Okay, we're not discussing that here and now." I pointed at him. "But we're most definitely doing it tonight."

"I'd love to do it tonight." His voice was downright husky.

I burst out laughing. When I got my breath back, I asked, "Have you always been like this? Did I just not notice?"

We both resumed walking up the path toward our office building. "I've always been like this," Denis said calmly. "I just don't show it to people very often."

He held the door for me and I went through the entry lock to hold the second door for him. As he passed me, I studied him, taking into account all the new information I had on him.

He was still the same guy, the guy I was slowly but definitely falling for, but he had a lot more layers than I'd thought. Somehow, I'd judged him in the same way that most people probably judged me. They just saw the timid and silent exterior we showed them in our everyday lives and never stopped to wonder if perhaps there was some more fascinating stuff going on on the inside.

Denis was definitely fascinating and I intended to get to know every side of him.

The door to our office was closed when I reached it, so I burst through it, assuming nobody was there.

Wrong assumption. Fidi and Tristan were both there and making out in the corner.

They flew apart at our interruption, both blushing furiously. Fidi flashed us a huge smile before going to sit down in his chair, while Tristan stood there, a hand over his eyes and head hanging low. "Sorry," he mumbled.

Denis chuckled and went over to shake hands with both guys before settling into his own seat.

I stood there, frozen for a moment, before finally forcing myself into action. If I didn't do this now, I'd never do it.

"There's something I need to tell you," I blurted out too loudly, making all three men in the room stop and look at me. "Shit. Sorry. I'm really nervous." I was hyperventilating.

Tristan gave me a tentative smile. "No worries. Would you like for us to find a meeting room for some privacy?"

I shook my head. Get it out, get it over with.

"I didn't steal the database." I was talking too quickly but there wasn't anything I could do about that right now. "But I'm dating Denis and that's why I was freaking out last week."

"Ooo-kay." Tristan stood stock still, staring at me with wide eyes.

Fidi broke into a huge smile and gave a thumbs up to both me and Denis, making both of us blush and squirm.

I took a deep breath. "I'm a bit crazy when it comes to protecting my privacy," I said. "So I freaked out about mixing my personal life with my professional one, and wasn't sure if I wanted my colleagues to know anything."

Tristan nodded and smiled. "*That* I certainly understand."

He'd been in the closet until very recently, so he *would* understand that part, even if it was probably for very different reasons. The end result was the same.

And if he'd been able to overcome his fears to own up to whom he loved, then so could I.

"Thank you for telling me, Laure," Tristan said. "I promise I won't tell anyone else on the team. Your personal life is your business and only you get to decide who knows what." He glanced at Denis as he said this, as if he was also delivering a message to him with his words.

"But I do appreciate knowing why you were acting so shady last week. I was seriously wondering if you'd somehow been involved in this whole database-for-sale thing." Tristan gave the most sincere smile I'd ever seen on the man. "I'm glad you weren't."

"Me too," I said without thinking. "Anyway…" I walked over to my desk and started pulling my laptop out of my backpack. "We will probably tell the rest of the team." I met Denis' gaze and took a second to assess all the emotions churning around in my chest. "But maybe not today."

Denis nodded in reply. "Don't worry," he said with a wink. "I won't do like the boss and kiss you in front of the entire team—not unless you want me to."

A groan from across the room made me break eye contact with Denis—my boyfriend!—only to find Tristan with his head in his hands. "How long is that going to be a thing?"

Fidi practically jumped with glee in his chair, the highlights in his hair catching the rays of sunlight slanting in through the window. "*Forever*, if I have a say in it."

The two started bantering but I zoned them out. To smile at my boyfriend.

"This is going to be weird," I said.

He grinned back at me. "Sounds great."

FORTY-FIVE

It Was Totally Realistic

I HUDDLED DEEPER into my pink blanket and adjusted my seat so that my laptop would fit comfortably in my lap. I had my herbal tea ready, flowery fumes licking their way out of my cup and into the room, my latest chapter had gone live less than an hour earlier, and I was ready to read the comments.

What more could a girl want on a Saturday night?

Oh, right. My boyfriend sitting across from me on the couch, his own laptop on his knees, and his own cup of herbal tea in his hand.

I hadn't slept in my apartment in over a week. Every morning, I planned to go back. Told Denis that I had to get a couple of things, check my mail, all that stuff. And every morning, Denis said that sounded like a great idea, and offered to take me by my place straight away, before we went to work, to get it out of the way.

Which meant I didn't have to go back at night—so I didn't.

And every morning, I thought of one more thing that I might need at Denis' place if I stayed the night, so I brought it with me.

My pajamas were here, half of my barrettes were here, my pink blanket was here.

Because Denis was here.

"Have you read the comments yet?" Denis asked.

"No! So don't tell me anything." I leaned over to look at his screen. "Are you reading the comments to *my* story?"

Denis rumbled a laugh and a happy frisson ran through my body to know that *I* made him laugh, that he was *my* boyfriend, and that I'd get to hear that sound every day. "I always read all the comments to your stories," he said. "Now hush, I'm trying to count the number of exclamation points on Tinkerbell98's comment."

"What!" I sputtered and almost spilled tea on my pink blanket. I wasn't sure if I was trying to put a hand over Denis' mouth so he wouldn't spoil anything else or if I planned to simply take off. In any case, the tea forced me to take a deep breath and not get ahead of myself. I gently placed the mug on the worn coffee table and opened the page for the writers' forum.

"One more word and I'll block you," I said.

"You wouldn't!" Denis' eyes went comically wide and he put a mocking hand to his chest, proving he knew I would never do that.

I ignored him and clicked on the comments for my latest chapter. Already over one hundred comments—not bad! I checked out Tinkerbell98's comment. "That's at least twenty exclamation points!"

Denis had closed his own laptop and put it aside. Now he came crawling across the couch to my side, paying attention to my laptop, but with his intent very clear in his beautiful brown eyes. "You deserved every one of them." He leaned in to kiss my neck right below my ear. "You're a very talented writer." A kiss in the spot where my shoulder met my neck. "You write very hot sex scenes."

He gently pushed my laptop closed and placed it on the table. I should have protested but I really couldn't care less about the rest of the comments right now. My brain took a backseat as my body took over.

"So you liked it?" I said and stretched out as best I could on the couch so Denis would get better access.

A hand found its way under my shirt and I gave a long exhale as a soft caress landed on my stomach and eased its way up toward my chest. Denis growled and brought his lips right in front of mine, his heavy-lidded eyes staring into mine.

"It was sexy as hell," he said. Shot forward for a quick kiss. Then another. "But I'm not entirely certain it's physically possible to do what your characters did in that scene." His eyes darting down to my lips, he gave me one more of his super-quick, non-satisfactory kisses.

I aimed for an offended huff but ended up on a breathless sigh. "Are you suggesting my writing isn't realistic?"

His lips curled up in a smile and I got a longer, more satisfying kiss. And then the bastard pulled back again, just when I was getting lost in it.

"I think it needs testing," he said, his voice and face mock serious.

"You want to test—" My breath caught as I replayed the last scene of my story in my mind. "The scene needs test—" I gulped and licked my lips. "You know what, I think you're right. That scene needs testing. Do you know of anyone who might want to give it a try?"

Denis' growl was most satisfactory. "I know just the right people."

FYI: The scene was totally realistic.

Author's Note

THANK YOU FOR reading Laure and Denis' story! If you enjoyed the book, I hope you'll consider leaving an honest review somewhere, to help other readers find the book.

I wrote a follow-up short story from Denis' point of view in March 2020. It's one of the rare lockdown stories I've written—as in, the characters are in lockdown—and I had lots of fun writing it. It will be available only through my newsletter, so make sure you sign up if you want to spend a little more time with Denis and Laure.

This story was first published in 2020 under a pen name. It seemed like a good idea at the time, but I've discovered I do not have the patience or will to have two social media presences, so I've decided to bring all my books under one name.

If you want to stay updated on any new stories, I invite you to sign up for my newsletter on rwwallace.com. You can opt in or out of the genres you're interested in, so you can get updates only on romance books for example, or add in mystery…you can even choose to get information (in French) about French translations!

R.W. Wallace
rwwallace.com

ALSO BY R.W. WALLACE

ROMANCE

FRENCH OFFICE ROMANCE SERIES
Flirting in Plain Sight
Hiding in Plain Sight
Loving in Plain Sight
(tie-in short story, available through newsletter)

MYSTERY

GHOST DETECTIVE NOVELS
Beyond the Grave

GHOST DETECTIVE SHORTS
Just Desserts
Lost Friends
Family Bonds
Common Ground
Till Death
Family History
Heritage
Eternal Bond
New Beginnings

THE TOLOSA MYSTERY SERIES
The Red Brick Haze
The Red Brick Cellars
The Red Brick Basilica

SHORT STORY COLLECTIONS
Deep Dark Secrets
A Thief in the Night

Short Stories
Cold Blue Eternity
Hidden Horrors
Critters
Gertrude and the Trojan Horse
First Impressions
Let Them Eat Cake
Out of Sight
Sitting Duck
Two's Company
Like Mother Like Daughter

Fantasy (short stories)
Unexpected Consequences
Morbier Impossible
A Second Chance

Science Fiction (short stories)
The Vanguard

Lollapalooza Shorts
Quarantine
Common Enemies
Coiled Danger
Mars Meeting

Adventure (short stories)
Size Matters

About the Author

R.W. WALLACE WRITES in most genres, though she tends to end up in mystery more often than not. Dead bodies keep popping up all over the place whenever she sits down in front of her keyboard. Except when a romance just *has* to come out. Or when a whole new fantasy world is taking form in her mind… You get the point.

The stories mostly take place in Norway or France; the country she was born in and the one that has been her home for two decades. Don't ask her why she writes in English—she won't have a sensible answer for you.

Her Ghost Detective short story series appears in *Pulphouse Magazine*, starting in issue #9.

You can find all her books, long and short, all genres, on her website: rwwallace.com.

www.ingramcontent.com/pod-product-compliance
Lightning Source LLC
LaVergne TN
LVHW041703060526
838201LV00043B/547